Little Ed & Golden Bear

Eligio Stephen Gallegos

Moon Bear Press

Little Ed & Golden Bear
Eligio Stephen Gallegos

Moon Bear Press

Printing History

First Printing........July 1993

The author gratefully acknowledges the inspiration of Rhonda Lunsford to write this book, and the fine editing abilities of Trebbe Johnson and Norie Huddle in bringing it to its present state.

All rights reserved.
Copyright © 1990, 1993
by Eligio Stephen Gallegos
This book may not be reproduced in whole or in part without permission except for brief passages for purposes of review.

For information address:

Moon Bear Press
Box 15811
Santa Fe, NM 87506

Library of Congress Catalog Card Number: 93-79099

ISBN: 0-944164-06-4

For Everyone
Who Is
Or Has Ever Been
A Child

Other books by Eligio Stephen Gallegos, PhD

Inner Journies: Visualization in Growth and Therapy
(co-authored with Teresa Rennick, RN, MA)

The Personal Totem Pole: Animal Imagery, the Chakras,
and Psychotherapy

Animals of the Four Windows: Integrating Thinking,
Sensing, Feeling, and Imagery

CONTENTS

The Ceremony of Severance	1
Wandertime	7
Little Old Grandfather	10
Ownership and Relationship	13
Removing the Sapwood	17
Orgtime and Lintime	19
Centering the Pole	21
The Four Windows	23
Laying the Pattern	28
The Window of Feeling	30
The Beginning Carving	38
The Window of Sensing	41
The Window of Imagery	45
Ceremony of the Animals	48
The Solar Plexus Animal	55
The Belly Animal	59
The Grounding Animal	62
The Throat Animal	67
The Forehead Animal	72
The Crown Animal	79
Conversations with Golden Bear	81
The Council of Animals	86
The Ordeal With Raccoon	96
The Transformation	100
Discovering Himself	104
The Golden Bear	108
Freedom and Slavery	116
Identity	120
The Totem Pole	124

Calling The Tree 132
The Event 136
The Passageway 140
Anora 143
The Gathering 147
The Flow 150
Wolf 152
The Final Carving 155
The Return 159
The Beginning 162
Author's Epilogue 170

The Ceremony of Severance

Little Ed had only recently arrived at this coastal village. Here the mountains seemed to spring straight up out of the sea and the small houses clung closely to niches in the earth. The surrounding tall cedars reached yearningly toward the sky.

He had always loved wood, its beautiful grain, its warm brown color deepening naturally as it aged, the smooth warm feel as he ran his fingers over it, its responsiveness to his carving knife. Wood that he had come here to spend a year or two learning about from one of the great master carvers. Now he was living in Golden Bear's home and learning skills from the woodcarver he most admired. He was excited.

The choice to come here had been his own. It could not have been otherwise. The year or two of Wandertime had been anticipated with great excitement ever since Little Ed could first remember. And at age twelve he had left home and undertaken the journey he was now on.

His feelings welled up large as he recalled the severance ceremony in the small community where he had lived. It had been the doorway to the largest experience of his young life. Tears filled his eyes as he remembered once again the large Hall of Ceremonies; it was beautifully constructed with massive wooden beams and it provided a feeling of strength and protection. The entire community was present. They had just finished the meal that they ate before ceremony. Then people had risen, one by one — Uncle Joseph, his mother's brother, had risen first, and he spoke about the first time he had met Little Ed the day after he was born. Uncle Joseph spoke about the shape of Little Ed's head and the feel of his skin and the depth and color of his eyes. He then spoke about the changes he had seen in Little Ed as he grew and matured. About the beautiful openness and receptivity he had always experienced from Little Ed, and his generosity. As Little Ed listened to his uncle he suddenly became aware in a different way, a new way, about himself as experienced by his uncle, and of the deep feeling connection that his uncle had for him.

When Uncle Joseph was finished he sat down. Then Tom, Little Ed's best friend stood up and told how he would miss him and spoke of some of the adventures and escapades they had been involved in. Many other people rose, one by one, said warm and glowing things about Little Ed, and then sat down again. He knew them all well, for in his education program he had spent days or weeks with each one, getting to know them in their homes and at their work, and they had discussed their interests and views of the world with him.

And finally it was time for the formal severance. Little Ed, his parents and his sister, Susan, entered the central circle of the Hall of Ceremonies. As they stood in that circle the community governor entered it and tied one end of a thick cord around Little Ed's waist and the other end around his mother's waist. The length of the cord allowed them to stand about three feet apart.

Their community governor, Mary Roberts, was a woman in her sixties, solid and warm, with a clear direct gaze. She had done her growing fully, pursuing her maturing directly and definitively as each event in her life had presented itself to her. She was well suited to the position she held as community governor and was loved and respected by all its members. Little Ed remembered her coming to their home shortly after his sister was born, welcoming the infant girl and expressing her joy that the community had a new member.

Now Mary Roberts tied a second cord around Little Ed's waist, measuring out its length with her hands and tied the other end around his father's waist. Little Ed felt the firmness and the heaviness of the cord.

And finally a lighter cord was tied around Little Ed's waist and the other end around his sister Susan's waist.

Mary Roberts now brought out a hinged wooden case. Holding it in her two hands, she said, "Little Ed, this community has watched you emerge and grow, and we have protected and cared for you as a child. We have taught you about ourselves and have supported you as you discovered your own nature and interests. Now we stand with you as the doorway opens into a wider world and we offer you our warmth and our love to carry with you as a part of your being as you go forth."

She opened the case and held it as Susan drew out the large silver shears.

His sister Susan looked into his eyes. "I'll miss you while you are gone. We've always called you Little Ed but I've always thought of you as Big Ed. I love you and I'll miss you." She then took the large shears and cut the cord that bound her to her brother.

Father held the shears next. He put his hands on Little Ed's shoulders and then bent his knees until their eyes were level. "You are my first born and I always had high hopes for you. I always wanted you to succeed where I felt I had failed in my life. I really wanted the best for you.

Now that I stand here ready to cut the cord I am aware that you need to find your life yourself, and to know what is right for you. I hope it is good and that you reach your wholeness. I love you, my son." Taking the shears he placed them around the cord and with more effort than he realized it would take he cut the cord. Tears were running freely from his eyes. He handed the shears to his wife.

Mother now spoke. "When I first carried you in my body I could feel how special you were and I loved the warmth that you brought to the core of my being. And as you grew in me I could feel myself changing. I could feel the earth carrying the potential of all that grows. I suddenly knew the meaning of the trees and of the flowers. I could feel the continuity of the animals and of all life throughout time, and I experienced myself as a beautiful passageway through which you could arrive.

"That evening when I knew it was time and we went to the birthing tub I could feel the entire universe holding me as I gave myself to being the doorway for your arrival. The water was beautifully warm and it seemed to massage me as my body pulsed in the rhythm of your birth. When you emerged you tried to swim away but the cord held you. I knew then you would be strong and independent.

"As I cut this cord now I know that the universe will

hold you and care for you, and that you will grow and develop into your own fullness. I love you." She took the shears and cut the one remaining cord that connected them.

With that Little Ed turned and ran out of the Hall of Ceremonies. He did not look back.

Wandertime

Little Ed remembered boarding the train for his journey to Golden Bear's village, his mind swarming with thoughts and feelings. He had not been prepared for the power of the feelings. Great surges of sadness suddenly welled up, spilling out through his eyes as memories of the warm events of his childhood presented themselves in review. But no sooner had he dried his eyes than the excitement of his journey would fill him to the point of shuddering.

"I really am doing it! I really am already on my journey," he would think to himself.

Then he would suddenly feel completly alone and think that he would never see his family and his community again. He was this little speck alone on the earth. He would disappear and no one would ever see him again. The excruciating aloneness.

But then he would feel himself held, really held by a warm and caring universe, the same universe that cared for the earth and the trees and all other people. Warmly, givingly, lovingly.

The train ride seemed to take forever, and at the same time he was there before he knew it.

"I know that what I'm doing is very important," he said to Golden Bear, "but sometimes I feel so sad. I miss my family. And I feel like maybe I'm not ready for this yet."

They were sitting in the carving shed that Golden Bear had built with his own hands. Wooden carving tools were perched along the walls in nice neat rows, suspended in racks above the two wooden workbenches. The smell of sweet, fresh wood permeated the room.

"These emotional pulls and tugs are entirely appropriate to the beginning of Wandertime. They are part of your growing," responded Golden Bear.

"But it's scarey. I feel...well, sometimes I feel like I'm all alone."

Golden Bear inhaled, long and deep, before he spoke. Little Ed had the fleeting feeling that Golden Bear was breathing in what he was feeling.

"You have left your first nest, just as a young bird

leaves its nest. And until you leave the nest you cannot learn to fly. Now you have come here to learn how to carve. You have left the nest of your family and you have begun to fly. Soon you will start to build a different kind of nest, one that you will share with the community. These feelings are an important part of the energy changes that are vital to your new being. You must allow that energy all the space it needs within yourself."

Little Old Grandfather

The straight trunk of a small cedar was lying lengthwise in the center of the carving shed. Without saying a word, Golden Bear took an axe that was standing in the corner of the room and handed it to Little Ed. Taking a larger one himself he motioned to Little Ed to approach the log.

They both stood before the log as Golden Bear spoke. "Little Old Grandfather," he said to the log, "I spoke to you when your feet were still rooted in the earth and I asked you to participate with me in the creation of a totem pole. You offered yourself willingly and we both knew that we were on the proper path. You have spent your life standing in the elements among your brothers, but now I have brought you to this little house. For the first time you are sheltered by a roof rather than by the sky. I ask you to be gentle with me here, to help me free your power so that it can be seen by all, to teach me who you are as we work together here.

"This is my young friend," he said, introducing the tree to Little Ed. "We will work together with you. We will honor you and treat you with all respect, and we ask you to tell us about yourself as we work."

With that Golden Bear lifted his axe and began stripping the bark away from the log. With his eyes and a movement of his head he motioned Little Ed to join in.

Little Ed felt a deep thrill that Golden Bear would trust him immediately to help with the large pole. He had expected Golden Bear to begin by telling him about all the tools, their various uses, and ways of handling and sharpening them. But now he watched as Golden Bear lifted his axe and smoothly cleared a small strip of bark away from the log. Sometimes the bark hung in shreds from the log but usually it was cleared cleanly with a single stroke.

Little Ed hefted the axe, feeling its weight, and it was heavy. By the end of the day he would feel a deep warm ache in his shoulders and back, but an ache that felt good. He made a tentative stroke at the end of the log opposite where Golden Bear was working. The axe bit into the bark and stopped. He looked at Golden Bear, who seemed to take no notice, and saw how he followed each stroke through, lifting the axe off the log at the end of each stroke. After a few more tentative strokes he felt his entire body, from his feet on up, entering into the stroke. The axe blade moved cleanly through the bark

He also watched as Golden Bear would get a great strip of bark peeling, putting down his axe and pulling with both hands until a long strip of bark had come off. Little Ed understood that the task was to peel the bark off the log in the most efficient way, and they both worked like this for several days until the log was smooth and clean.

Ownership and Relationship

Golden Bear took a seat in a large old comfortable chair and Little Ed perched himself on a nearby stool leaning his back against the workbench.

"This is a difficult time for many people in the world," said Golden Bear, "because the world is in the process of the Great Shipshift."

"What is the 'Great Shipshift'?" asked Little Ed.

"For many many years some of the people on this earth have lived in terms of an idea called 'ownership.' Now, there's nothing wrong with living in terms of an idea as long as that idea fits with the way the universe works," began Golden Bear in what would be a rather lengthy answer to Little Ed's question.

Golden Bear didn't mind taking all the time he needed to answer questions, for he considered each question to be a new step forward by the mind, and the mind of a young and receptive boy like Little Ed deserved the sure footed guidance that a mature elder could give. And Golden Bear knew that his answer would become a major thoughtnode in the eventual working of Little Ed's mind.

"But this idea, 'ownership', does not work the way the universe works; it only works the way a certain limited part of people's thinking works. So it was bound to arrive at the edge of its limits somewhere along the way. People did not realize that ownership traps them in a frozen place in the world and keeps them from growing into their fullness."

"But I don't understand," said Little Ed. Certainly I own the clothes I brought with me and my own set of carving tools. How can these keep me from growing?"

"Oh," replied Golden Bear, "you certainly need your clothes to keep you warm, and those beautiful carving tools will definitely help you discover new dimensions of yourself. I'm glad you brought them along. But if you think that you own them then you are sadly mistaken. You have the use of them for a while but your tools will become worn and you will outgrow your clothes. So at best you have use of them for a short while as you both grow and change"

"Is there something wrong with owning things?" asked Little Ed.

"The difficulty with the idea of ownership is that it calls your attention in a certain way: It moves you into a position of control and protection or defense; you feel you have to control that which you own and if it were to be taken from you, you would feel as if a part of yourself had been lost. Then you would feel diminished and become sad. Or you would become angry and determined to get it back. That would just lead to conflict.

"Ownership is a stance with all of the automatic actions that go with defending. Defending separates people at the boundary and what the world needs now is communion."

"But what would we do if we didn't own things?"

"If we didn't own things we would have to come into a relationship where we could use them mutually. The stance which the universe supports is that of *relationship*. And you must enter into a relationship with all of those things that you think you own: with your clothes and particularly with your carving tools. You see, a relationship is an ongoing event, it is not cut and dried like ownership. In relationship there is communication and ongoing disovery, and thus the likelihood of growing. Relationship demands a fluid awareness and sensitivity, whereas ownership kills awareness by freezing it into a fixed position.

"You must learn to talk to your clothes and your carving tools and listen closely for their answers. Let them tell you about their individuality and uniqueness. Let them tell you what it's like to be carried about and used by you. In that way you can learn things about yourself that you never would otherwise."

"I see," said Little Ed. "When I'm in relationship I have to take into account where the other person is, or what's going on with my tools, or my clothes. Owning is kind of a way of excluding other people and of neglecting my relationship with those things I think I own."

"Exactly, my friend," said Golden Bear. "So the Great Shipshift is the change that is occurring right now all over the world, from ownership to relationship. There have been many people who have lived in terms of relationship rather than ownership but they have seldom been understood because of the way that ownership blinds the awareness of people who live in ownership. Those people who have lived in terms of ownership are now seeing that it kills some of their own aliveness, and that relationship nurtures their aliveness. People are changing ships at this time, difficult though it is, but there is no other choice now because ownership has begun to kill the earth."

Removing the Sapwood

With the bark cleanly stripped off, Little Ed had thought they would now begin carving, so he was surprised when Golden Bear took a large adze from the corner and handed it to him.

"Now that the bark is removed we must clean off the outer layer of white sapwood," said Golden Bear, "until the log is softly rounded and dressed only in red wood."

"I have never used an adze before," said Little Ed.

"Hold it with both hands and swing it toward you," said Golden Bear, taking a few strokes as instruction. "There is a smaller adze that can be grasped with one hand, and we will use that later."

Whereas the blade of the axe had been parallel to the handle, the blade of the adze was perpendicular to the handle, similar to that of a hoe, only the adze was strong and heavy, with a slight curve to the edge of the blade.

Little Ed watched Golden Bear swing with smooth even strokes, removing a small chip of white sapwood with each stroke. But he found that when he swung the adze it lodged itself in the wood and he had to work to remove it.

"Let yourself feel the stroke with your body," Golden Bear advised, "rather than trying to do it with your thinking. Your body itself already knows how to do the work. Let it come back to its own way of knowing."

He found himself surprised at Golden Bear's words and felt himself stumbling over his own understanding.

"Your thinking wants you to make the perfect stroke, at the very beginning, but this is a familiarity that your body needs to come to know in its own way. It needs to feel its way into a kind of recognition and remembrance."

Little Ed suddenly realized that he was trying to please Golden Bear, to show him how much he already knew, rather than trusting that he had come here to learn and that Golden Bear accepted him exactly where he was. He found that if he let himself *feel* Golden Bear's movement as much as see it, that his own body would begin to make slight motions, especially his shoulders and arms. He realized that his own arms and hands felt good holding the adze, and if he allowed his entire body to move, to be involved in the swing, the movement was easy and the stroke was clean.

Orgtime and Lintime

"As you find your own rhythm in carving," said Golden Bear sitting in his comfortable chair, "you can shift the cord of connection to Orgtime and away from Lintime. You need the support of Orgtime as you begin your journey of independence and relationship with the universe."

"What is Orgtime?" asked Little Ed. "I've never heard of it before."

"The best way to explain it is by comparing it with Lintime," answered Golden Bear. "Lintime is the time the clock tells you about. Or the calendar. It is the same for everybody. But Orgtime is something that is unique to each living being.

Golden Bear went on to explain that for thousands of years some people tried to substitute Lintime for Orgtime as if that could be done. "Lintime is the same for everyone and refers to the relationships between changes that happen in the universe. For example, the earliest measure of Lintime used to be the passage of the sun through a day. But this passage varies with the seasons and is also very close to Orgtime, so when this was the measure, then Orgtime and

Lintime were closely aligned. Later, people began using the pull of gravity as a measure of Lintime, for example, how much water or sand would run from one container to another if there was only a small opening between them. Some people still use this method for cooking eggs. And with the discovery of mechanical gears and springs Lintime was even more highly refined and broken down into smaller units. Lintime became even more mechanical. Ultimately the rate of the vibration of a crystal or the rate of emission of radiation were used as measures. Now the reason all of these changes could be used as measures in the first place is because they are all related to each other, and so Lintime is really a measure of the relationships between ongoing changes in the universe. By the use of Lintime people were able to coordinate their actions with precision.

"The difficulty with all this measurement was that it left out the individual. One always had to go outside of oneself to know Lintime. Orgtime, on the other hand, requires that you go deeply inside of yourself, and know about the changes that go on inside of you and of your own personal relationship to the universe. To know within yourself when something is right for you regardless of what Lintime says. Orgtime is more like a rhythm, like your breathing or your heartbeat. It happens in its own way in its own time and it is like a dance. Your own Orgtime, Little Ed, is faster than that of most people."

Centering the Pole

It had taken many weeks to clean off the sapwood. Golden Bear had instructed Little Ed about adzing around knots in the wood, finding the direction of the grain and flowing with it in his movements so that his adze would not chip out a large chunk. In working Little Ed found that he would come into a rhythm that would carry itself, where his movements were fluid, with a fullnes and a grace that felt more like a dance. And it felt like the log itself was guiding him in his strokes.

By now all the white sapwood had been removed. The log was covered with a soft pattern of adze strokes and the red cedar of the wood was fully exposed. Little Ed understood that the appearance of the log displayed its relationship with the two men, and that it was one of softness, care, and beauty.

"Now we must lay the center line," announced Golden Bear. "Once the center line is laid it will guide the emergence of the pattern and hold the carving in balance."

Together they turned the log and Golden Bear positioned himself first at one end and then the other, scanning the log, assesing the number of knots on the various surfaces and finally settling on the side which contained the least. He then gauged the centermost part of the upper surface and drove a small nail at one end. To this he attached a string which he stretched to the other end and moving it slightly back and forth he came to the center line of the pole. He tied the other end to a nail driven into the opposite end of the pole, so the string was stretched taut. Golden Bear now plucked the string in the center and snapped it once. Little Ed was surprised to see a small puff of light blue smoke emerge from the length of the string. Then he realized the string had been powdered with chalk. This left a strong line down the entire length of the pole's center.

The Four Windows

"One of the most significant ceremonies in life and the one vital to the growspurt from dependence into independence is the Ceremony of the Animals. But before I take you to meet your animals you should know about the four windows," said Golden Bear with an attitude of deep warmth but great seriousness. Little Ed could feel from the sound of his voice that he should listen attentively.

"There are four windows through which we can experience the universe and develop a relationship with it. When we are born all of these windows are combined into one, so we really don't make a distinction between them. But they also develop at different rates and as they change, we change. But the real reason for needing to know about them is so that we will not confuse them with one another. People who confuse them with one another develop a misunderstanding of the universe and of their own relationship with it."

Little Ed had no idea what Golden Bear was talking about.

"Take this moment right now," said Golden Bear

aware of the confusion in his young listener. "The only way I can reach you to help you sort out these four windows is through the window of thinking. Thinking is one of the major windows people have and they have developed it to an extent that no other animal has. All animals think, but only people have a window of thinking that is so big that they can easily get lost in it and never be found again."

Little Ed laughed at the thought of this.

"In fact," continued Golden Bear, "universities used to be staffed by many people who were hopelessly lost in the window of thinking."

Little Ed became more attentive at hearing this, and an event from his childhood began to come back to him. Little Ed had, in fact, lived near a university. Late one afternoon he had been playing on the sidewalk in front of his home. It had been a warm day and he had been lazily watching a line of ants as they followed their trail across the sidewalk to a large grasshopper that lay dead in the tall grass. He was intrigued by the fact that the path the ants followed was not straight even though there were no obstacles on the sidewalk, and even when there was a gap and only a single ant was on the path, it still followed that same curving trail to the grasshopper. Suddenly he lurched aside to avoid being stepped on by a tall man heavily dressed in a wool suit who even then didn't appear to see him. The man was muttering something to himself and did not even turn around when Little Ed yelled at him to be careful. Little Ed had never understood this event until today.

"People who are lost in the window of thinking can neither see nor hear," said Little Ed, more to himself than to Golden Bear.

"Oh, most of them can see and hear," replied Golden Bear, "but just as soon as they see or hear something they immediately translate it into thinking! The only way things can reach them is by going through the window of thinking, so the universe they experience is totally dependent upon the thoughts that are available to them. They 'think' they are experiencing the universe, but they are only experiencing the patterns imposed by their own thoughts."

Something else now began to become clear to Little Ed.

"Why would a person get lost in the window of thinking in the first place?" he asked.

"Most people who get lost in the window of thinking do so without ever intending to," answered Golden Bear, "but they begin by using thinking as a way of avoiding fear.

At first it may be only minor: when in a frightening situation they may exprience a slight sense of relief when their attention moves away from fear and focuses on thinking. But as they do this more and more, thinking gradually gains power over them and becomes their only escape until finally thinking is surrounded by fear and must be maintained as a preoccupation in order to avoid the ever present fear.

"These people then become terrified at the mere thought that thinking might come to an end. So the need for continuous thinking is buoyed up by all kinds of reasons. By now their only way out of being lost in thinking is to be willing to plunge into the fear. This plunge always feels like a dying, so few people are willing to take it voluntarily. It is in fact a dying; it is the death of the story they have been compulsively telling themselves about who it is they think they are."

Little Ed sat silently absorbed in a deep realization.

"To talk about the power of fear brings us naturally to the window of feeling, but before we go there I want to say a few more things about the window of thinking," continued Golden Bear.

"Thinking is a magnificently beautiful window. It is so fine that many people become completely enraptured with it. Many people, seeing its great beauty, have thought that it must be the foundation of the universe. Now, thinking is certainly the foundation of the 'thought' of the universe, but thinking itself is just one of the flowers that grow in this mysterious universe.

"Thinking has been vital for us to know the intricacy of the universe, and also for us to be able to begin to sort out the functions of the four windows, and it allows people to know each other in great intimacy by the fact that they have learned to turn their thoughts into sounds and marks which they can share. Thinking, and the sounds of thinking, began as a way people had of telling their stories to one another, and stories are the fabric of people being together. In this way people enter each others' lives deeply and appreciatively. But it also allowed people to attempt to hide from one another, by refusing to share their thoughts or by deliberately distorting their stories.

"Thinking is remarkably intricate, but in actuality, thinking is still so simple that it works basically by dividing everything in two."

Laying the Pattern

Golden Bear removed a large drawing that had been hanging on the wall of the carving shed. The several large sheets of paper were covered with strong bold fluid lines. Little Ed suddenly understood that this was the pattern for the animals that would be carved on the pole.

Glancing at the pole, then gauging its length with his outstretched arms, Golden Bear began laying out the patterns along it. Beginning at the top he carefuly positioned one of the pages in relation to the center line and traced the pattern onto the log but only on one side of the center line. He then suddenly flipped the paper over and traced the same pattern in reverse on the other side of the line. In this way the design was absolutely symmetrical from one side to the other.

With a wave of his head and a sparkle in his eye he motioned Little Ed to come over and stand opposite him on the other side of the pole. Golden Bear then placed the paper containing the next design beneath the first one, and again carefully placing it in relation to the center line he traced it on one side then flipped it over and handed Little Ed the grease pencil. Little Ed was surprised and pleased that he would be brought into the actual laying of the design and firmly traced the other side of the design Golden Bear had traced. In this way they moved quickly the length of the log, each tracing the design on his own side of the center line until the design was completely traced along the length of the log.

The Window of Feeling

"The window of feeling is very mysterious and difficult for us to talk about because, as you may have guessed, in order to talk about things we must look through the window of thinking. So we can *talk* about the window of feeling only to the extent that it lends itself to being accessed by thinking. The problem with this is that thinking has developed primarily by looking through the window of sensing, where things can be seen. And since feeling is invisible the words we have available for talking about it are limited.

"Feeling is the awareness we have of energy. And everything is fundamentally energy so everything has a feeling to it. There is a feeling of the energy of the events and people around us as well as a feeling of our own energy. And if we refuse to feel some of our own energy then we become either blind or confused about the energy that is around us.

"For a long time, through what is called the Emotional Dark Ages, some feelings were forbidden and childeren were trained very early to hide the forbidden feelings. So they grew up with tremendous amounts of hidden energy; usually it was hidden so well that even they didn't even know it

30

was there. Then a brave man named Freud began to discover those hidden energies in people, and he found that the path to the energy was through imagery. Most people treated this as a curious event, and were ashamed and horrified to think that they might have some of those hidden energies. What is really curious is that people were not shocked at the time to realize that they were so divorced from their wholeness that there were large parts of them they didn't even know existed. The question that should have been asked by everyone, in outrage, was 'How is it possible that I have been so unaware of such a large part of who I am? What ever happened to me that this is missing?' At least then they would have acknowledged that something very serious was going on.

"But most were quite afraid to leave the window of thinking, and so they argued about the missing part and speculated about it without ever visiting that dimension themselves. One would think they would have set out immediately on an exploratory mission, just to take stock of what was there, but even most of those who professed to be guides to that lost realm preferred to do so from the comfortable position of their own window of thinking. Very few were actually willing to accompany someone on that journey.

"There was a time when venturesome people used

plants or chemicals to help them make that journey, but this was usually abrupt and sometimes disastrous because there were no good guides and they could not determine their own pace. It is through the relationship with the animals that the journey became safe, systematic, and true to each individual.

"Can you imagine the strangeness of that time? It was as if someone were to suddenly become aware that people have legs and feet! The strange thing is not that we have them but how could we have forgotten? How could we have gotten so far away from a relationship with our feet that someone else has to discover it for us?

"So the Ceremony of the Animals is a totally natural ceremony that is vital to the relationship with who we each are; it helps us come back to that place where we are in continuous relationship with the deepest parts of our wholeness.

"But to get back to the window of feeling. Feeling is the energy of our aliveness. We are aware of it as it comes to us and it also energizes us to be in relationship with other other beings, the world, and the universe.

"The universe itself is energy! And so our position as living beings is to be aware of the energy of the universe."

Little Ed had been hearing this with a sense of rapture, but one question kept nagging at the back of his mind. Suddenly it came to him clearly and he asked Golden Bear, "I know that I see with my eyes and taste with my tongue, but what part of me is it that feels?"

"It is your entire body that feels!" answered Golden Bear. "But there are some parts of you where feeling is more concentrated than in other parts. Your belly, for instance, experiences feeling more than your back. And your hands more than your forehead. As you develop the ability to enter more and more fully into the window of feeling you discover that your whole body is like a landscape of feeling with its own particular slopes and contours, its own springs and deserts. But after awhile you become aware that the landscape is also the landscape of the universe.

"For example, when you see something, you don't think about your eyes. You are too busy looking at what you are seeing. It is not a time to be preoccupied with the part of you that is seeing. All of you sees through your eyes, just as all of you feels through your body.

"One more thing," added Golden Bear, "besides being invisible, the other curious thing about energy is that it is continuous. It exists as a continous flow and therefore we have difficulty knowing where one energy ends and another begins. In this way, through the window of feeling, all things are continuous. All things are unified. All things are one. And this is one of the places that our knowing about the different windows is essential: because in the window of sensing things seem separate, as also through the window of thinking. So to know the universe in its entirety, in its wholeness, all windows are essential!"

Little Ed was exhausted just from listening to Golden Bear. But he also knew that he didn't have to try to remember all Golden Bear had said. He had already learned that there was something in him that did the remembering, and that it would re-present those learnings at the times when they would be needed as long as he did not interfere.

By now it was time for dinner, so Little Ed and Golden Bear returned from the carving shed to the small house where Golden Bear lived with his wife, Anora. Little Ed's room was also in this small house.

Anora was a warm and deeply settled woman. Little Ed always felt good around her. When he was with her it was as if she embraced him with her warmth and held him on her lap even though they were sitting in different chairs just talking. He immediately felt relaxed as they entered the kitchen where they took their meals. She greeted him warmly with a smile and a nod as he sat down at the table.

As they closed their eyes while Golden Bear gave thanks to the Great Spirit, as he did before every meal, Little Ed became aware, as he never had before, that he could feel the presence of Golden Bear's wife. It was difficult for him to describe the experience to himself. There seemed to be a golden glow where she was sitting, and it was larger than her physical size. The feeling had a greater density in the area down the center of her body, like a large glow-worm. He felt/saw something else as well: a golden arm that connected her belly to his.

Little Ed was lost in amazement about this new way of seeing when he suddenly became aware that Golden Bear and Anora were already eating and so he opened his eyes and joined in. Throughout the meal he felt a contentment he had not felt before, like a warm, settled glow deep within himself. And he saw a sparkle in Golden Bear's eyes, as if Golden Bear knew what he had just discovered and was happy for him.

After dinner, when they had returned to the carving shed, Golden Bear turned to him and said, "As you saw at dinner, seeing through the window of feeling looks different from seeing through the window of sensing. Remember that all energy is light, and feeling sees this light in and around everything. But you must also be relaxed in order to see through the window of feeling. If you are afraid or angry then that will drive you to see and act in a very narrow way; it may be handy in emergencies but for the most part we are partially blind when that happens. Can you believe that there was a time when people were deliberately trained to close the eye of feeling and not use it for seeing? That people were trained to be deliberately blind?"

Little Ed had trouble believing that people would deliberately be trained to limit what they were capable of and he told Golden Bear as much, yet he was also aware that there was much about feeling that he was just beginning to discover.

"Yes," continued Golden Bear, "it is only recently that we have begun to emerge from the Emotional Dark Ages! The human animal is capable of such infinite learning that it has been difficult for teachers to refrain from teaching students things which were taught only for the convenience of the teacher. Can you believe a teacher would train a student to have limitations just so the teacher's job would be more convenient? To be still when it was time to act? To curb the students' awareness so that it would only be focused on what was handed to them rather than following their awareness so that they could discover its own path? But of course I'm talking about teachers who themselves had never achieved the fullness of their own growing, teachers who themselves had been trained to be tremendously limited and to only follow a mechanical path. But that was a time when teachers were only viewed as conveniences rather than being honored as the ones who help people grow into their wholeness."

The Beginning Carving

The months of preparation of the pole had gone easily and smoothly. Now the carving of the figures was to begin.

But first Golden Bear spent some time with Little Ed going over the animals that had been sketched onto the pole and pointing out the way the lines of the figures flowed into one another, so that even though there were individual animals, they were all in essential relationship to one another. The eagle at the top of the pole was grasping the ears of the bear below with its talons, yet there was a place where talons and ears were indistiguishable from each other. And the paws of the bear could have been also the paws of the beaver that it was holding in its lap. The legs of the bear were also the ears of the rabbit at the base. So the animals were inseparably joined in relationship.

Handing Little Ed a large chisel and a mallet made of alder wood, Golden Bear then began chiselling out large chunks of cedar just beyond the edge of the pattern drawn for the eagle.

"Don't be afraid to go too deep," said Golden Bear.

"The worst that can happen is that you come out on the other side!" he added with a chuckle.

Again, Little Ed was awed by the trust that Golden Bear had in him. He placed the chisel near the leg of the bear and whacked it with the mallet. He felt good at this initial cut and continued moving the chisel until the leg was outlined a slight distance outside the pattern. He then placed the chisel further out and a large chunk of red cedar flew out. He continued in this way until the leg of the bear stood out beyond the underlying wood that he had removed.

"Continue to raise the bear in this manner," Golden Bear said to him, until he has emerged fully. And you can also talk to him, ask him to instruct you in places that seem difficult, invite him to help you with his own birth."

"Big Bear," Little Ed whispered, "please help me with your birth. I want you to stand forth powerful and strong. You are holding many animals in your lap and on your head, so you need to be strong. Work with me now so your body can come forth, and later I will ask for your help on your paws and face."

As he spoke his chisel seemed to move more freely and knowingly. He found himself using the mallet with more confidence and ease, and the fragrant cedar chips flew at an increasing pace. Golden Bear looked pleased.

As the days passed the bear stood out more and more prominently. Then Golden Bear selected the one-handed adze and brought it to Little Ed.

"Now you can begin rounding the bear out. This will give him more of his final shape."

Little Ed took the smaller adze and began to softly hack away the corners that the chisel and mallet had left. He found the wood responsive to his strokes and very quickly the bear began to assume a softer, rounder presence.

The Window of Sensing

By now he had roughed in the carving and Golden Bear had come over to show him the use of the small knives. One was straight and the other had a soft curve to it. These left a different, finer pattern on the wood.

"Your job is to help this animal to see," Golden Bear said with a twinkle in his eye. "You have already helped him to come into his form in the wood but form is only the beginning. The form has come into this world so that it can see the world around. So when you carve the eyes, be aware that you are helping them come forth in order to see. And notice how this fellow also has eyes in his chest. His chest and his heart also need to be able to see. An animal sees with everything he's got!"

Little Ed seemed to see the bear in its wholeness for the first time. Rather than being made up of parts, it had a central wholeness and all the parts participated in and held a relationship with that wholeness. As he continued to carve with the knives he felt almost that the bear's wholeness was directing the placement of the cuts.

"The third window through which we can experience

41

and develop a relationship with the universe is the window of sensing. Some people for a long time called that which we experience through the window of sensing 'reality', and some people still do. Of course reality is experienced through all of the windows and the use of the word 'reality' only for what was seen through the window of sensing shows the bias that has existed in our thinking.

"The window of sensing is vital for our initial survival, but we have recently gone through a time when people were so intensely focused on survival that they became rigid and incapable of completing their wholeness. The purpose of survival is to come to the place where we can continue to grow into our totality. At that time survival has to take a back seat in our thinking.

"It is through the window of sensing that we encounter the beauty of the universe as well as the terror of it. We do need to avoid dangerous places for our survival, the places where we could be injured. But at one time injury and fear were used as a major aspect of education and what that did was to freeze people in a focus on survival. Much of what was done in the name of 'education' was really a way of making people more rigid rather than of providing them a place where they could explore and develop their own uniquely individual dimensions to the fullest. Children were forced to follow the dictates of the teacher rather than listening to and trusting their own deepest knowing. It is good that things have changed since then."

Little Ed felt a deep ripple of emotion from Golden Bear as he spoke

"The human animal is a remarkably tender animal, especially when it is first born, and if there are not others around to care for it, it will not survive, so inclusion within a group is an essential aspect of safety and survival. But exclusion from the group came to be used as one of the most subtle and consistent ways of punishing people for not learning. And what was demanded to be learned was not something that could be enlarged and continually built upon, but it was usually the rote repetition of particular thoughts and phrases. It was presumed that equality meant everyone doing the same thing. It is only recently that people have learned that equality means each person growing to his fullest capacity. People are naturally social, but many of the rigidities that were created through education actually made people feel bad about who they were because their own original dimensions were ignored and they came to feel excluded from being a necessary part of the larger group of human animals."

Little Ed listened respectfully to what Golden Bear was saying while his knives continued to be guided by his emerging sense of the bear's wholeness He had the feeling that Golden Bear had exprienced something deeply painful in what he was now talking about.

The Window of Imagery

In working with the finer detail of the pole, Little Ed had become enchanted by the small faces that were parts of the bear.

"This bear has faces in his paws," he said excitedly.

"It is good that you have seen that so soon," replied Golden Bear. "As you help those little animals to come forth and see, you help the bear itself to come into its aliveness and to experience its own wholeness as well as the fullness of the world around."

Little Ed continued carving with a renewed fascination while Golden Bear continued to speak.

"In order for you to meet your own Council of Animals we need to go through the window of imagery. The window of imagery is vital to our welfare, for it is the window that governs growing and healing.

"I told you earlier that thinking works basically by separating everything in two, and the window of sensing also readily sees things as separate, but it is only the window of imagery that knows how to bring things back into their wholeness. That is why it is the window of growing and healing.

"For many years people denied that the window of imagery had any validity, because they always thought it should work exactly like the window of sensing, and if something was experienced in the window of imagery which never happened in the window of sensing then they would become either frightened or else they would say it was invalid. They never asked what the window of imagery was about and they never went on journeys just to explore its dimensions. The closest they would allow themselves to it was to marvel at some of the creations that had emerged from other people's imagery.

"And some tried to use it in a very controlled way, demanding that imagery follow the dictates of thinking. They thought of it as a tool, demanding that people hold the same images or that images follow a certain prescribed order, rather than recognizing it as one of the most mysterious and marvelous windows through which we are allowed to have a relationship with the universe.

"For it is through the window of imagery that what people call magic actually happens, and the greatest magic is the magic of our own healing and growing.

"It is in the window of imagery that something can be both itself and its opposite simultaneously, or can be totally continuous and fluid. Or you may see yourself as you are now, as you were as a child, and as you will be as a grown man, all at the same time.

"Since it is impossible for these things to happen in the window of sensing, people called them illusions, denied their validity, and used the window of sensing as the standard to which the other windows were forced to conform.

"So people lived blindly for many, many years, denying those aspects of themselves that could have brought them into a relationship of wholeness with the universe.

"The saddest part is that as each child was born he was taught to distrust these dimensions of himself, to laugh at them or hide them or be afraid of them, rather than to welcome them and value them and learn to explore them to their fullest extent.

"So we take this journey to your animals as the beginning step in a journey to your wholeness."

Ceremony of the Animals

Little Ed was surprised when Golden Bear stood up and asked him to sit in the large comfortable chair where he had just been sitting. For some reason he had thought they would go to a place similar to the Hall of Ceremonies where he had undergone the Ceremony of Severance.

"The Ceremony of the Animals is one of the most personal ceremonies you can ever undergo and it could take place almost anywhere. The main requirement is readiness. Many times the animals themselves have tried to begin the ceremony, but the person wasn't ready, or didn't know how to be in relationship with them. Sometimes the animal comes and the person just says 'I wonder what that means?' rather than saying 'hello' and welcoming the animal. You can imagine how the animal might feel at that. What if you went and knocked at someone's door and they opened it and looked at you and said to themselves, 'I wonder what that means?' and then closed the door and walked away? Would you feel like coming back?"

Little Ed laughed at the thought of it. Golden Bear chuckled.

"The animals are a dimension of the universe that require respect whether we encounter them through the window of sensing or through the window of imagery. If we have a respectful relationship with the animals, then we will have a good relationship with ourselves and with other people.

"The world has recently come through a period of time where people were deliberately taught to disrespect themselves, to hide part of who they were and feel ashamed of it. Out of this they then felt disrespect for each other and for parts of the universe, so when they encountered these parts they felt they had to destroy them. The council of animals ensures that we live in harmony with who we are and therefore with the entire universe.

"If you nurture the animals that you will soon be meeting, you nurture your relationship with the universe."

By now Little Ed was yearning to go meet his animals and he hoped Golden Bear would soon finish what he was saying and get on with it.

"Each animal will be met through an energy doorway in your body. There are seven of these doorways. Sometimes in intense situations you experience the doorways themselves, for each doorway is a particular living energy, a specific dimension of your aliveness. For example, I know that you felt some of these doorways when you first came to see me."

As he said this Golden Bear looked at Little Ed with a penetrating directness and Little Ed felt himself move with a start as he remembered walking into Golden Bear's workshop for the first time.

The last leg of his journey to Golden Bear had required that he take a ferry boat, as no trains came to this village. After asking directions at the dock he had walked up the long trail and Golden Bear's wife, Anora, had greeted him. She had seen him through the kitchen window and as he raised his hand to knock at the door she had already opened it and invited him in. Little Ed remembered the warm glow that he had felt in his belly at this. After placing his two bags in the small room where he would be sleeping, and drinking the cool glass of water that Anora offered him, he left the house and walked the short distance to the shop. Even as he approached the shop he felt something strange in the area between his belly and his neck, something like pressure suffused in warmth which then intensified as he walked through the doorway and saw Golden Bear for the first time.

He felt that same sensation now as Golden Bear looked at him. Golden Bear smiled gently.

50

"The two major doorways through which you feel my energy are your heart and your solar plexus. These may be the best places for us to begin."

Even though he had waited so expectantly, Little Ed now felt a slight dread at not knowing who he was going to meet or even if there would be anyone there.

"Close your eyes and let yourself stand in the doorway of your heart," said Golden Bear softly but firmly.

Little Ed could feel his heart pounding and his breathing intensify.

"Now, call out within yourself and ask if your heart animal would be willing to come forth. Then just wait and watch. Never try to force the animal or to demand anything of it. You have to be willing to let it come on its own terms, in its own time, in its own way. All you can do is extend the invitation and be willing to be fully present with it no matter what it may be."

As he called out in his mind and invited his heart animal to come, Little Ed found himself thinking of the long path from the dock up to Golden Bear's house. He remembered the strange rustling in the bushes he heard when he was out of sight of the village. He had thought at the time that it might be a wild animal and now he found himself at that same spot on the path. Hearing the rustling he stepped off the path and peered into the underbrush.

"Here I am, over here," said a strange voice that drew his attention to a dark opening beneath a blackberry bush. Peering into it he saw a fat little bear cub sitting back comfortably in a cozy damp hollow under the bush, pulling a branch loaded with ripe blackberries to its mouth.

"Are you my heart animal?" Little Ed asked without thinking.

"Yes. It's me. Come share some of these delicious berries with me," said the cub.

Litle Ed found himelf crawling into the hollow that had apparently been scraped out by the cub, feeling the cool warmth and the cozy protected nature of this secret place. He sat next to the cub, sitting back like the cub and pulling a branch loaded with blackberries to his mouth, eating the berries directly from the branch. They were sweet and juicy.

"This is my secret place," said the cub. "I always feel good and safe when I come here. I wanted you to know about it so you can come here sometimes, too. The blackberries are always ripe here."

Little Ed felt a warmth of shivers flowing through his body as he recognized the deep kindness of this bear cub in its willingness to share its secret place with him. He wished that he could offer the bear something, too.

"What can I give you?" he asked the cub.

The cub thought for a moment although he didn't stop chewing the delicious berries and then said, "Tell me the truth."

Little Ed felt a sickening lump in his throat as he heard these words and he was plunged into a memory of something that had happened three years ago. He had taken a small enamelled pin from his sister's room and when she could not find it his father had asked him if he had taken it. He said he had not and his father said sternly, "Tell me the truth!" He continued to deny having taken it but as he did he felt a strange tightening in his throat and a flushing in his cheeks. The next day he buried the pin in the garden. He had felt uncomfortable about the incident ever since. There was something puzzling about it, and he had tried not to think about it. In fact, he had forgotten it totally until this moment. He told the cub all about it and cried freely. The cub put its arms around him and licked the tears from his cheeks. Little Ed felt his throat relax as he heaved a final sigh. It felt so good to be held by the cub and to tell him what had happened.

"What was on the pin?" asked the cub.

"I don't understand," said Little Ed, feeling puzzled.

"What was on the pin?" repeated the cub.

With a jolt, Little Ed remembered the pin clearly. It was an enameled silver pin of a bear cub.

The Solar Plexus Animal

"Ask the cub if anything more needs to happen right now," said Golden Bear.

Little Ed felt startled by Golden Bear's voice but yet it seemed to belong perfectly in what was happening. Sitting in the cub's cozy shallow burrow, he turned to him and asked, "Cub, does anything more need to happen right now?"

"No," said the cub, "but thank you for coming to see me. Even though I am only a cub I am also very ancient. Come visit me again." The cub gave Little Ed a warm embrace.

"Say goodbye to the cub and allow yourself to leave him easily and gently," came the voice of Golden Bear.

"Goodbye, Cub. Thank you for sharing your secret place with me," said Little Ed.

"Now, position yourself in the doorway of your solar plexus," continued Golden Bear, "and call out within yourself and ask your solar plexus animal to please come forth."

Focusing his attention in the area half-way between his heart and his navel, Little Ed called silently into himself, "Solar plexus animal, are you there? Would you please come forth?"

Little Ed heard some rustling in the leaves and thought he must still be with the cub but just then he saw a shiny nose and two penetrating eyes. "Are you my solar plexus animal?" he asked.

"Yes, I am," answered the intensely curious raccoon. "Come, there's something I want to show you."

As Little Ed followed the raccoon he recognized something of himself in the animal: the quickness, the intensity, the alertness and curiosity all seemed to touch places in himself where he felt a kinship.

"You're a lot like I am," said Little Ed.

"No, I'm not," replied the raccoon abruptly, much to Little Ed's surprise. "I'm much neater!"

By then they had reached the raccoon's home under the roots of a dead tree.

"Come in and see!" said the raccoon in its intense and precise voice.

Little Ed crawled through the opening and found himself in one of the neatest little dwellings he had ever seen. Everything was sparkling clean and precisely in its place. The sparkling quality reminded him immediately of Golden Bear's carving shop, where every tool had its place. "If you put everything where it belongs then you'll know exactly where it is when you need it," he remembered Golden Bear saying. But the raccoon's home reminded him of something else as well. He could see his own room in his parents' home: clothes were strewn about, a half-finished model space station was on his desk, shoes were tossed here and there, and he could hear his mother's voice saying, "Now, why can't you keep your room neat and clean like your sister does?" He felt his face flushing as he remembered her words and felt himself becoming angry at the raccoon with all its cleanliness.

Turning suddenly in the raccoon's home he tipped a chair over. The raccoon just watched him as he he apologized, embarrassed, and righted the chair again. But as he stood up he brushed against a picture on the wall and it crashed to the floor. Embarrassed even more, he noticed the raccoon staring at him with its strange piercing gaze. As he grabbed the broom from the corner of the room in order to sweep up the broken glass from the picture frame, the end of it struck the chandelier, smashing it and sending broken pieces throughout the room. Little Ed felt like a trapped animal and frantically lunged for the door, tipping over and smashing other pieces of furniture on his way. He could hardly breathe, feeling suffocated by the raccoon's once neat home, and ran as fast as he could to get away. As he escaped with his life he could feel the raccoon behind, staring with those piercing eyes.

Little Ed thought he noticed Golden Bear chuckling softly. Then he heard his powerful voice saying, "Thank the raccoon for being with you and allow yourself to leave it easily and gently for now." But Little Ed was already far away from the raccoon, still panting from his narrow escape.

The Belly Animal

"Stand in the doorway of your belly, just below your navel," said Golden Bear, "and call out within yourself, 'Is my belly animal here? Would you come forth, please?' "

Little Ed still felt he could sense a smile on Golden Bear's face, but before he could think any further he found himself looking at a spider face to face. He was lying on the floor and it was strangely dusty. There was something immediately above him and he suddenly realized he was under a bed. His bed! And he was only four years old. His eyes hurt. He was angry and sad. The spider looked at him with the same direct gaze that he had seen in the raccoon.

"I know how you hurt," said the spider, "but you can be here with me."

"I'm angry at you also," Little Ed heard himself replying. "I'm angry at everybody! I'm angry at everything!"

Little Ed now became aware that he was also watching this scene as well as reliving it, and he was fascinated by what he saw. Feelings welled up as he remembered: his mother and father had just returned from the birthing center.

He had wanted to go with them but they had left him at home with his aunt. She tried to talk to him, but he was filled with the thought of the birth, intrigued, curious, and hurt that he had not been allowed to go along. He had spent the afternoon straightening his new room and making it neat like his mother did, thinking how pleased she would be when she returned. But when she returned, she hardly paid any attention to him, instead lying in bed holding the new baby. He felt hurt and angry and ran and hid under his bed.

Little Ed found himself crying and crying upon remembering this, and thinking also about what a good friend his sister had become, and of how she loved him, and how he had enjoyed introducing her to all the new things in the world. He thought of her words at the Ceremony of Severance, how she had called him 'Big Ed' and how full he had felt.

"You buried that hurt long ago," said the spider, "and you've carried it long enough. Now you can let it go. Come! There's something I need to show you!"

As the spider climbed up its web, Little Ed found himself following, and was amazed at how spongy and resilient the web was. As he gripped the web it felt like the web also gripped him, and he bounced along behind the spider as if on a trampoline.

Then he found himself in a long, web-like tunnel, and the spider was far ahead, so far ahead that it looked like something sparkling. As he hurried toward it it got larger and larger and he suddenly realized it was coming toward him, and it was not the spider but a white horse, with wings, galloping toward him with its hooves just barely touching the surface of the tunnel. Little Ed was overwhelmed with feelings.

Little Ed could hardly contain himself as the horse lowered its head and Little Ed climbed on its back. The horse flew out of the tunnel and high into the sky. Far below Little Ed could see the curve of the earth and all the green forests and rivers covered by the openness of the sky. The beauty of this expanse filled him, and his breathing became strong and firm.

The white horse then flew him back down toward earth, heading straight for the village where Golden Bear lived.

The Grounding Animal

"Thank the white horse for the transformation he has just gone through and for the new space he has taken you to and just allow yourself to leave him for now," said Golden Bear.

Little Ed watched as the white horse flew away, feeling a deep gratitude for this fine, powerful, gentle animal. And feeling also a strange new indescribable freedom. His breathing came easily and full.

"Stand now in the doorway of your pelvis and call forth for your grounding animal," said Golden Bear.

Little Ed didn't know what a grounding animal was but he could feel himself standing in his pelvis, facing inward, and calling, "Grounding animal, are you there?"

A rabbit poked its nose out of a burrow in the earth and glanced around quickly. Seeing Little Ed he held perfectly still and just looked at him.

"Are you my grounding animal?" asked Little Ed.

"Yes, I am," replied the rabbit.

"Do you have anything to tell me?" asked Little Ed.

"Come closer," said the rabbit.

Little Ed moved toward the rabbit, then he stopped.

"No, still closer," said the rabbit softly.

Little Ed moved up until his nose was almost touching the rabbit's nose.

"Let yourself move into me," said the rabbit.

Little Ed felt strange at this suggestion, but for some reason he continued to move toward the rabbit until suddenly, like being swallowed, he was inside the rabbit. No. It was more than that. He was the rabbit.

He could feel his nose twitching and scanning the air for "things." The things had a body and a substance to them, but the substance consisted of a tangible, dense fragrance, as if he could taste the "thing" through the air. He then felt himself rise up out of the hole and lope easily toward one of the "things." The "thing" became more dense and attractive, and he found himself chewing on the leaf of a green plant. It was deliciously succulent, and its juices had a strong and interesting flavor, like sudden chlorophyllic explosions. Little Ed was curious at how natural this all seemed, the movements of the body, the chewing and swallowing, but what was most curious was that the air itself was a fragrant landscape of "things." He couldn't seem to find any other word for these "things" because they seemed to exist in a dimension that was totally new for him.

As he munched away at the delicious flavor, he noticed that his long ears were constantly moving, scanning the area for sounds, and that the sounds had a different quality from any he had ever heard before. There was a precision to them and a clarity and a fullness, as if each sound were three dimensional, with both a surface and an inside. But there was something else, a transparency — no, not that. Oh, yes! That was it. Each sound held a particular feeling quality. There was the sound of the soft wind which swept around him in patterns and soft swirls, an air landscape in which the other sounds were placed with precision. The soft, swishing movement of grasses, rhythmically moving back and forth, which felt comforting and soothing. Then there were the crisp, sudden sounds, like darts, at which his head and body came immediately into stillness, and he "looked" in that direction with his ears. He realized that his ears and nose could see better than his eyes, and much farther. And they could see around things. No. (He was having trouble finding words for these new dimensions of experience.) Things that would have been in the way of seeing with his eyes were transparent to seeing with his ears and nose.

Something else was curious as well. At the same time that his body was relaxed and at ease, there was a readiness for movement that he had never before felt. The place of his ease existed at the very edge of a potential for movement in any direction, at any moment, but without fear. Or, better said, what he might have called fear as a human became a natural part of the energy of movement in the rabbit, and itself "moved" the rabbit, almost as if the rabbit were being squirted out of a toothpaste tube by these energies. Awareness, the extensive multi-sensory landscape, the rabbit's feelings and movements, were all one fluid totality. Little Ed felt centered and at-home like he had never felt before.

Now he was outside the rabbit again, looking at the rabbit with a deep feeling of love and appreciation. "You're beautiful!" he said to the rabbit, not having the language to express the intricacy of what he was feeling both for the gift of knowing the rabbit's experience, and also as a way of saying that the rabbit's very existence was a continual, fluid work of art.

"Yes," said the rabbit, "and you must search until

you find the place of beauty in yourself. It is there, waiting for you to come home to it."

Tears came to Little Ed's eyes and he cried freely.

The Throat Animal

Golden Bear waited, feeling the deep connection Little Ed had made with his grounding animal, waited caringly until the tears were over and the deepening energy had done its work.

"I'm sorry," said Little Ed.

"No!" replied Golden Bear immediately, in his full, warm voice. "Never treat your crying as if it should not be part of who you are. Crying is good! It washes your soul and gives depth to your being."

Little Ed felt warmed by his words and sensed the fullness of the place his crying had let him feel.

"Thank the rabbit for having allowed you this magnificent experience," said Golden Bear, "and ask it if anything more needs to happen at this time."

Little Ed replied that the rabbit told him this was enough for now but that they needed to have other visits. Little Ed felt a sense of soft excitement as he looked forward to further visits with this magical animal.

"Leave him then, and let yourself stand in the doorway of your throat," said Golden Bear. "Now, call out within yourself and ask for your throat animal to come forth."

Little Ed felt a quivering in his own throat. "Throat animal, are you there? Will you come to see me?"

Little Ed suddenly found himself in a forest facing a large old oak tree. "Are you my throat animal?" he asked the tree, surprised at even hearing himself speak like this. To his further surprise the tree answered. It had the deep settled voice of an old man who had weathered many years and still stood firm and strong.

"No, I am not your throat animal," answered the tree, "but your throat animal does live in me."

As the tree spoke, Little Ed felt a vibration in his very bones, a deep tickling of his marrow that connected him with the earth itself. He felt that the tree knew him through and through, like an ancient grandfather whom he had finally come to meet.

"I would love to spend more time with you," said Little Ed, "but I am supposed to meet with my throat animal."

Just then a beautiful full melody emanated from the branches of the tree above Little Ed's head. He looked up to see a small bird perching on a branch.

"That was a beautiful song," he said.

"Thank you," answered the bird.

The bird was so high in the tree and so small that Little Ed had trouble seeing it. Even though he peered and tried to focus, he still could not see it well.

"I'm having trouble seeing you," said Little Ed.

"Yes," said the bird, "you have never seen me fully. You have only seen fleeting parts of me. You have never seen me in my wholeness."

"I don't understand what you mean," replied Little Ed. "I've only just met you."

"No, I have been with you for a long, long time," answered the bird, "but you hardly ever let me sing my song!"

The bird sounded angry and Little Ed flinched at

this. "You hardly ever let me express my anger," said the bird.

Little Ed was confused. "How do I keep you from expressing your anger?" asked Little Ed. "I have nothing to do with your anger." By now he was beginning to get a bit angry himself.

"It is by your fear of my anger," said the bird. "Your fear is a constraint within which my anger is forced to live, and it's not comfortable in here."

Little Ed's confusion grew. How could his fear keep the bird from doing what it would do? He didn't understand.

"Every experience should be expressed truly," continued the bird. "When you hold back one experience because of another, you are not allowing me my full song. If I am going to be me then I must sing my song fully regardless of who is listening, or even if no one is listening. My song is to be sung. It cannot to be pared down because of how it might be heard by others. I cannot modify my song because of people's inability to hear, or because of their obsession with interpreting. That would only cripple me."

Little Ed could hardly believe what he was hearing.

The bird made sense even if Little Ed did not understand specifically what it was talking about. There was a warm feeling of something melting in his throat.

"Little bird, I want you to sing your song fully," said Little Ed, not even knowing where his words were coming from. "And if I do something that interferes with your song, please let me know right away."

The bird then sang the most beautiful song Little Ed had ever heard. The mellow fullness of its notes and the extent of its scale surprised Little Ed, and its versatility was astounding. Little Ed could only listen in fascination. The song ended in long true notes of remarkable clarity which seemed to penetrate Little Ed's heart. Or was it that they emanated from his heart?

The Forehead Animal

Little Ed listened as the bird's song faded imperceptibly through time and space. He did not know how long he had been listening when suddenly Golden Bear's voice broke through the stillness.

"Ask the bird if there is anything else that needs to take place at this time."

"Does anything else need to take place right now?" asked Little Ed, seeming to address the silence in the tree.

"No," replied the little bird immediately in its crisp, clear voice, "but don't forget your promise. I will let you know just as soon as you try to confine my song!"

"I will remember my promise," said Little Ed solemnly.

"Thank the bird for being with you. Now, let yourself stand in the doorway of your forehead," said Golden Bear, "and invite your forehead animal to come forth."

Little Ed felt his attention move to the center of his broad forehead and he could hear his inner voice saying,

"Forehead animal, are you there? I invite you to come forward."

He was surprised to find himself still facing the tree and thought that his meeting with the bird must not have been completed.

"Little bird, what do you want? I need to go visit with the forehead animal," he said impatiently. But there was no answer.

"I am who you seek," came the quiet thunderous voice of the tree.

Little Ed could not have been more surprised. "But you're not an animal! How could it be you?"

"All that exists is alive," said the tree, "so why differentiate so precisely?"

"Do you mean things like rocks are alive, too?" asked Little Ed incredulously.

"Are the nails on your toes and fingers and the hair on your head any less an essential part of your aliveness than the skin on your nose?" replied the tree. "This universe is one living organism and every part of it contributes to its aliveness."

"But I don't understand how you or I could be essential to its aliveness. Certainly my death would not change the universe?"

"Both your life and your death are essential to it," answered the tree. "Each red blood cell in your body is essential to your aliveness, though there are many of them, and each is here for a particular purpose, just as you are."

"What is my purpose, then?" asked Little Ed with great interest.

"Just as the red blood cell does not ask its purpose but carries it out anyway, so must you. It is not your purpose but your questioning that is in question," answered the tree enigmatically.

"But . . . but . . . but. . . " stuttered Little Ed.

"Questions are more numerous than anything else in the universe," said the tree, "but that does not mean they are always appropriate. A question is useful when it opens the door to a quest. It is destructive when it interferes with the silence necessary for understanding. The problem with your questions is that you are given to try to answer them immediately, and this gets in the way of being able to sort out valuable questions from useless ones, for they all grab you with equal intensity."

Little Ed could feel his head filled with the energy of questioning but no words appeared in his mind. So he just listened.

"Feeling that a question is important just because it is a question is the major illness of human beings. You must allow your awareness to grow until you can see the true concern behind each question. Only then will you be free from the automatic need to provide an answer."

Little Ed had difficulty believing that a tree could be talking about these matters. "I didn't know trees could think," he said, thinking aloud to the tree.

"Everything can think," answered the tree without hesitation, "but only people become addicted to thinking. Thinking is the anticipation of a direction. People want everything to be so secure that they spend most of their lives anticipating and very little of their lives experiencing. Yet they hunger most for the experience of being who they are."

"But isn't thinking valuable?" Little Ed managed to

ask.

"Thinking has tremendous value, but not as a substitute for understanding," answered the tree.

"How is it that you know so much?" asked Little Ed.

"I know because my roots are anchored firmly in the earth as my branches reach for the sky, and I drink freely from both."

"I feel as if I could talk to you forever," said Little Ed.

"That would be highly unfair to the other dimensions of who you are," answered the tree. "I gain my health from your wholeness and you from mine. Wholeness can only come from the full inclusion of the totality of who you are. To favor one aspect of yourself over another would invite imbalance and I need your balance. Rather than becoming preoccupied with only a part of who you are, find your true center and sit there in full receptivity."

Thoughts were whirling around in Little Ed's head but something deep within him had understood what the tree had said, and he felt remarkably solid. Something in him felt as firm a connection with the earth as the roots of the tree. And even though his thoughts were spinning around wildly he experienced a clarity like the sky into which the branches reached.

"I value your counsel," said Little Ed, "and I ask that you continue to advise me as you have."

"I will," answered the tree.

"Is there anything I can do for you in return?" asked Little Ed more in politeness than out of thinking that there might really be something he could do for the tree.

"There is something you can do for me, but not in return," answered the tree. "To do something only in return would mean that we are bartering and our relationship is limited. Doing something because there is a need, with no thought of repayment, is a way of caring for the universe of which you are a vital part."

"What is it you need from me?" asked Little Ed, feeling a deep love for this wise old tree.

"I need for you to water my roots freely with the tears of your heart," answered the tree.

Little Ed was totally surprised at this request and

although he did not feel like crying, he suddenly felt the trees words tugging at his heart and throat. Tears poured out of his eyes. His body heaved in great sobs. These were not tears of sadness but of deep joy. Little Ed felt a warmth, a glowing love for this tree and for the universe with which it connected him so profoundly.

His tears fell on the ground around the base of the tree, soaking down to its roots, and the tree emitted a great sigh.

The Crown Animal

"Thank the tree for being with you and allow yourself to leave it for now," said Golden Bear when Little Ed's tears had abated. "Then position your awareness right at the top of your head and call out for your crown animal."

"Crown animal, are you there? Would you please come forth?" said Little Ed as he felt his awareness hovering over his own head.

After patiently waiting for a considerable length of time, Little Ed found himself looking over a vast green valley. It was remarkably still. Nothing moved in it. Little Ed called out again, "Crown animal, are you here?"

A remarkably soft but full voice answered, "Yes, I am here."

Little Ed glanced around, expecting to see some physical entity. But he saw nothing. "I don't see you," he said.

"I am the sunshine that fills this valley where your animals and tree live. I am always here, warming and giving light," continued the voice.

Little Ed had encountered some difficulty with the tree speaking, but to think that the sunshine could speak required an extra leap. He was trying to locate it in a particular position. Could it really be everywhere in that valley?

"Your thinking may have some difficulty acknowledging me, but I nonetheless exist," said the sunlight, as if to allay some of Little Ed's consternation.

"I don't doubt that you exist, but how can you speak when you're so scattered about?" replied Little Ed.

"I am unified by my sameness, even though I may be found in many different places," answered the sunlight, "and by the fact that I have a single origin. It is because of me that your animals and tree can live. And in the final view, I also live through them."

"Is there anything I can do for you?" asked Little Ed, not believing that he could do anything at all for the sunshine. He was totally surprised by its reply.

"Let me shine through you!"

Conversations with Golden Bear

Little Ed had wanted to talk at length with Golden Bear immediately after he had met his animals, but Golden bear felt that it would be better if Little Ed were to spend the rest of the evening in silence, "to allow things to cook."

The next morning Little Ed was bursting with questions about the animals and he felt a radiant connection between himself and Golden Bear, but Golden Bear was warmly quiet. In the shop Golden Bear handed him the small carving knife he was to use and then with a staccato wave of his hand pointed to the animals on the pole. Little Ed felt a ripple of feeling run up his body and suddenly realized that the animals were positioned one above another just like the animals he had met yesterday in his own body.

As they began carving, deepening some of the incised lines and refining some of the details, Golden Bear began to speak.

"You must learn to go within yourself for answers, rather than to someone else. Not that there is anything wrong with asking someone else. There is not. But when we are young so many of our questions are answered by someone else that it then requires some effort to turn inward and let our own being author its own answers and flow in its own direction. People have recently gone through a long period of time when they were taught that the only valid answer had to come from someone else, from the 'authority', but that view abandoned oneself as being an essential element in the universe, and so was disrespectful. If we don't first respect ourselves, then our respect for others will always be incomplete."

Little Ed, initially so full of questions about his animals that he had difficulty hearing Golden Bear, suddenly found himself listening through a kind of inner depth.

"The animals that you met last night will be the guardians of your wholeness, especially once they have met in council, and so they require your respect. They are all power animals, and they are all good for us regardless of how much we may initially fear or hate them. In fact, when we encounter one that we fear or hate, that is the greatest challenge for us to enter into a relationship with our wholeness. For you it is now your solar plexus animal, or animal of action, the raccoon. There are ways in which your action has not been clear or clean, although that may have been taken care of through the transformation of your belly animal. The belly animal is the animal of emotion and passion, and when it changed from the spider that you met under your bed at age four into the flying white horse, a deep clearing happened in your emotions. The animals are the key to your growing and healing. They come from wholeness and so they know that dimension intimately.

"Your rabbit was indeed beautiful, and it is a doorway for you to know the universe on its own terms rather than those that you would try to impose on it. It is the key to going beyond the limited experience of yourself. The experience of the universe as itself is indeed magnificent and as you saw there is no way that words can meet it at that place. They can only try to catch up later.

"Your bird is already at home in your great tree and some day it may teach you how to fly. Letting it have the freedom to sing its own song is the first step toward flying. And the tree is at home in the sunshine, so here you have an incipient wholeness already at work. Your council meeting will be easy."

"But is the tree really real? I remember the spider, but I have never seen such a magnificent tree, and especially one that can talk, and so profoundly, at that," gushed Little Ed in an outpouring of pent up questions.

"Memory is but a narrow band of the window of imagery, and to place our acceptance of what is real in such a narrow space keeps us from knowing what imagery has to tell us about the universe. It is as if we would reduce the window to our own personal history rather than letting it carry us beyond that narrow dimension of ourselves. We must be willing to venture forth beyond the confines of who it is we think we are if we are to do our existence justice and fulfill our being in the universe." Golden Bear spoke with an intensity that Little Ed had not heard before. "The tree is real, and perhaps more valuable to you than any tree you have ever seen."

Golden Bear's words seemed to open a door in Little Ed to some indescribable feeling, a way of knowing that held limitless potential, a mystery that invited exploration and adventure, and a settledness within himself that seemed to defy belief. Something in him felt as solid as the earth.

"These animals (and within this he included the tree and the sunshine) seem to know me better than anyone ever has," said Little Ed. "Even the raccoon knows me in a way that I don't even want to see myself."

"They will be your principal allies on your path through life and death. It is because they know you so well that they can be the best guides available to you. They are all essential to your wholeness even though you may prefer some over others."

"When will they meet in council?" asked Little Ed.

"After they have cooked you a bit more," replied Golden Bear with a chuckle.

The Council of Animals

One evening after dinner, Golden Bear told Little Ed they needed to return to the carving shed. It was exactly six days after Little Ed first met his animals.

"Usually I would wait seven days but since your Orgtime appears to be six rather than seven, today is the best day to meet with the council of animals," Golden Bear said.

Little Ed's heart began to beat more rapidly at hearing these words. He had thought much about the animals and their significance, and he was particularly fascinated by the great tree and the sunlight. He had longed to meet with all the animals again and might have tried to on his own were it not for the deep respect he felt for Golden Bear.

"Have the animals come to visit you during these six days?" Golden Bear asked.

"No, they haven't, " replied Little Ed.

"If an animal should ever visit you on its own, if it should suddenly appear to you even in a dream, greet it first and then ask if it has brought you a message. For thousands of years people have generally ignored their animals and so have not been receptive to all the messages that animals bring. During that time the world became rigid and mechanical and it almost died. But during my lifetime more and more people have begun to care for the life of the world and to assume responsibility for the relationship that such caring requires," said Golden Bear solemnly.

Little Ed knew that the world had undergone significant changes in recent times before his own life began. As part of his Expansion Program he had gone through the Brief Human Story portion in the Interactive Visuals Library. He remembered now being horrified at the depictions of what children were forced to go through, the thing called "school" in which their movements were severely restricted and their interests, rather than being allowed to develop at their own pace, were determined by a single person in a stilted and mechanical manner. His own Development Program involved several adults and some older children who helped him focus on the evolution of his own abilities and qualities and to explore their development.

Reading and writing had come very naturally to him, especially through the use of the writescreen. This small, flat panel displayed pictures of all sounds, at least those that people spoke, and it could be set to do so in cursive or in block pictures. Little Ed had enjoyed watching it as people spoke, particularly his parents and sister, and also himself, so that recognizing the pictures of the sounds soon became second nature to him and it was a minor step for him to begin making those pictures himself. The pictures, even though he could make them with great ease, felt strange to him, and he referred to them as "silent speaking." He then learned that there were vast stores of silent speaking and that the beauty of silent speaking was that it could reach far across time and space. In fact, his family had a cupboard containing several shelves of small laserdisks which contained all the silent speaking that had ever been done. He knew that the silent speaking had at one time been contained in bulky "books" because his family still had shelves full of them, and he did enjoy reading these from time to time. But he also knew that the laserdisks in the same room contained the equivalent of enough books to fill several vast buildings. He had always felt that at some future time he would go into these volumes seriously, especially with the interactive visuals guides.

Little Ed's most enjoyable exploration however, had been in learning to make things with his hands. His hands always seemed to have a life and intelligence of their own, and they loved making small objects, especially ones that had a delicious feel to them, a certain smoothness or texture that communicated a particular quality. Little Ed loved to feel the objects he had made. Some were out of stone, some out of plasteel, but he had particularly liked to carve out of wood. In fact that was what had led him to select Golden Bear as the elder with whom he would work for the year or two of wandertime.

"The council of animals is one of the most important developments in coming into wholeness," said Golden Bear, "for this is the time when all your energies begin to return to their full and fluid communion, and sometimes these energies have been apart for many years. People can only be whole if all their energies have full access and can communicate readily with all other energies. The council of animals ensures that we have a means of coming back to that wholeness.

"One thing you should know before you go to meet with the animals in council is that they allow you participation as an equal. Their principal job is to grow you fully and they do allow you to have a say in that growth. But you must be willing to be fully present with them from wherever you are. If you think they are wrong in something you must tell them so, but you must also listen to what they have to say about it. Growing emerges from the relationship that you enter into with them, and to grow fully you must be willing to enter into a full relationship. They are not your servants, nor do they belong to you. You do not own them.

If you treat them like servants they will withhold their energy from you and you will suddenly find yourself flat and listless.

"They are skillful and intelligent in their own ways and they will use these qualities to help you grow. And as you grow they will allow you to participate more and more in the skill and intelligence which they share. As you grow they will gradually include you in the dimension from which they come. But in order for that to happen you will have to cease clinging to the dimension from which you have so far derived your identity."

Little Ed had absolutely no idea what Golden Bear was talking about but he listened respectfully.

"There was a period of time, when people were first rediscovering this dimension, when they felt that they were supposed to reprogram the dimension of imagery. They didn't understand that the dimension from which they sought to do the reprogramming was much less capable than the dimension they were trying to reprogram. It was as if someone were trying to teach Picasso to paint by numbers. Finally the vast creativity and intelligence of that dimension was recognized and people began to allow themselves to learn from it. They ultimately recognized that it was the place from which they themselves took form and began to honor it appropriately and to allow themselves to be imbued with its inherent qualities. Coming into wholeness requires a rebalancing of all of the components of who we are. We may be surprised to find that our lives have been greatly askew."

Little Ed was yearning to meet with his council of animals. "Can't we go and meet them now?" he asked. "What you are telling me makes no sense to me whatsoever."

"You are right. I am talking more about things that I need to hear than you do at this time," said Golden Bear with a glint in his eye. "Come, sit in this big, old comfortable chair again."

Little Ed seated himself in Golden Bear's chair. It was soft and cozy, and still warm.

"Close your eyes and give yourself permission to relax deeply," said Golden Bear in his full, sonorous voice. "Now place your awareness at the very top of your head and invite your crown animal to come forth."

"Crown animal, I invite you to come forth," said Little Ed when he could feel his awareness at the top of his head.

He immediately saw the wide, green valley. It was

filled with sunshine. The sunshine was happy.

"You feel happy today," he said.

"Yes," answered the soft, full voice. "I am feeling warm and beautiful with such a lovely valley to hold me."

Golden Bear's voice came through. "Ask the sunshine if this would be a good time to invite the animals to meet in council."

"Would this be a good time for the animals to meet in council?" said Little Ed.

"The time is perfect," answered the sunshine. "Call and invite them to come."

Little Ed called out through the valley: "I invite the animals and the tree to come together for a council meeting."

He immediately found himself at the foot of the grand, old tree. The sunshine was filling its branches and leaves with a magnificent golden light. The bird was singing softly in its branches. As Little Ed looked around he could see the other animals making their way to the great tree. The bear cub was shuffling along the path toward the tree carrying a twig of the blackberry bush with blackberries still on it. Raccoon came up through the forest, and when Little Ed looked he saw the raccoon's clear, piercing gaze and felt a pressure in his own solar plexus. The flying white horse flew down from the sky, landing at the foot of the tree, and the rabbit scampered in from the underbrush. The animals formed themselves into a circle and the bird flew down to sit on a branch at his position within the circle. The tree was to the north. Little Ed was also in the circle, at a position directly opposite the tree. To his right was the raccoon and to his left was the bear cub. The flying white horse was to the east and the rabbit to the west. Sunshine filled the entire circle.

"Greet them and thank them for coming to the council," Golden Bear's voice was full and rich, "and then say anything else that you need to say to them."

Little Ed looked around at the animals with a feeling of great love in his heart. "Thank you for coming to this meeting," he said. "I want to thank you for the growing that you helped me with when we first met. I know you each did something specific to help me grow, and I have been feeling much more solid since that day. Some of you, like tree and bird, gave me direct advice, and it feels good to know that this advice is available to me wherever I may be even if no one else is around. Something feels very sure about it and I want to ask you to please give me whatever advice you see I need at any time. I promise to listen.

"And with most of you, it just felt good to be with you. There are things I don't understand about the place that you live. Like how the spider became the white horse. Or how I was able to become the rabbit. And raccoon, I am still scared of you and I don't really trust you. You feel unpredicatable to me.

"I want to grow as much as I can. The little taste of it you have given me has been delicious. And I ask for your help in my growing. I also want to offer you my help in any way I can. I don't know what it will be like living with you as a family, but I'm excited. Thank you again for being here."

Little Ed experienced a deep, warm feeling in his belly. There was a sincere appreciation for these animals just being who they were, and also a solid sense of security knowing that they were his allies. He could feel now that there had always been an indescribable loneliness until he met the animals. A loneliness for them even though he had not even known of their existence. Now he felt whole.

"Ask them if they would be willing to consult among themselves and see if there is anything that needs to happen at this first meeting." Golden Bear's voice was warm and caring.

Little Ed asked them.

"The only thing that needs to happen here is between you and me," said the raccoon.

Little Ed's body tensed. He felt very afraid.

The Ordeal With Raccoon

Little Ed was face to face with the raccoon and he felt like turning and running away. If he had been alone with the raccoon he would have done just that. But there was something about the presence of the other animals that made him feel a responsibility for staying and facing whatever needed to be faced. The fact that he didn't know what needed to be faced or why he was afraid of the raccoon made him feel a bit crazy.

Raccoon took a step toward him, looking at him with his strange, steady gaze, and Little Ed took a step back.

"Remember, I am here with you, too," said the cub.

Little Ed looked at the cub who was still holding the small branch of uneaten blackberries, and felt a warmth from him. He then looked back at raccoon.

"Come closer and look into my eyes," said Raccoon.

Little Ed felt himself take a step forward although he still wanted to run away as fast as he could. He looked into

Raccoon's eyes and felt a shudder run through his body. There was something almost unbearable in the directness of Raccoon's stare. Little Ed became vitally aware of the black mask that Raccoon was wearing and of the fact that the mask did not hide the coldness in Raccoon's eyes.

"Let yourself enter into my eyes," said Raccoon.

Little Ed felt dizzy. Going into Raccoon's eyes was the least thing he wanted to do. As he entered into those eyes he felt something well up in himself and then was totally surprised at the shriek of agony that came as his entire body shook with great spasms.

He didn't want to see this. This could not have happened. No! No! No! But there he was, looking over the edge of his sister's crib. She was only a few months old. As he watched her, so small and helpless, a strange feeling began to come into him, a cold, sharp feeling. But it was the thoughts that he most wanted to run away from, to deny their very existence forever, to obliterate them and send them as far away as possible. The thought that he could easily kill this little girl and then he could have his mother's love and warmth all to himself again. The thought terrified him and he tried to bring up a barrage of rules and bulwarks against it. He tried to cover it over and pile things on top of it, but whatever he did there was no denying now, it was there.

Little Ed was horrified that he could ever have thought such a thing. He felt he was capable of being a cold-hearted murderer at the age of four. His body wrenched in convulsions as he cried out, NO! NO! NO! NO!

Finally, he just collapsed and sobbed for a long, long time.

When he finally began to stir, realizing that he had been quiet for some time, he became aware that he could feel warmth and fur all around. The animals surrounded him. They were holding him and stroking him with great tenderness. He opened his eyes and looked at them, half expecting to be condemned for what he had just realized he had thought about at the age of four.

Instead, the cub said to him, "You were really hurt by your mother's absence, when she was no longer there to hold you. It's too bad you didn't know us at the time. We would have held you."

"Yes," said the white horse, "you could have talked to us about it and we would have helped you understand."

"He still can," chimed in the little bird, to everyone's

delight.

Little Ed felt their soft caring, and to his surprise the bird was now much larger.

"I didn't even remember that had happened," he said.

The Transformation

Little Ed could feel his legs shaking as he sat up. The animals were around him, supporting him. He could feel their warmth and caring. He looked at the raccoon and was surprised to see that its mask was now gone. It looked different, as if something had changed about it. Its eyes were no longer frightening, they were warm and open, and it seemed larger somehow.

"I was so afraid of those thoughts!" said Little Ed.

"Thoughts must have their free range," said the tree in its deep, anchored voice. "Thoughts are only possibilities, and they can help us see the likelihood of certain outcomes. But thoughts must live with the totality of our being. What we do has to come from our wholeness, and if thinking knows this, then it can be more relaxed about its influence. Thinking is not supposed to be in charge. It is only supposed to lend advice. This is why it is so vital that all of who we are participate fully in what we do. After all, your fear itself saved you from the coldness of your thoughts. Now that your thinking has grown larger than it was at the age of four, it is time that this frozen place in you should melt."

Little Ed heard the trees words with a sense of great relief. It was not that he was a murderer! After all, he had not murdered anyone. His thinking at the age of four had merely taken the most direct and immediate route to the return of his mother, speculating that if his sister was gone he could then have his mother back. He felt that he had given his thinking tremendous power by being afraid of it and he said this to the animals.

"Your fear of this thinking was a time of growing power, it is true," answered the tree. "In order to act you had to have enough energy to overcome the fear, and so your energy had to develop quite powerfully. But now it is time for your thinking and actions to work in harmony and your fear prevented this. In order to heal, you had to go back through your fear in a healing direction."

The other animals nodded in agreement and added that one more thing still needed to happen. "Come with me into the center of the circle," the raccoon said to Little Ed.

The other animals formed a circle around them. The sunshine then streamed directly into the animals and tree forming the outer circle. Here each one of them focused the sunshine and aimed it directly at Little Ed and Raccoon in the center. Little Ed, at the hub of this wheel, could feel himself filling with sunshine and could see that Raccoon was also. It felt like all of the animals were giving him their energy and he could feel something melting and growing in his solar plexus. Just then Raccoon disappeared into a puff of smoke. Little Ed was quite surprised and as his eyes tried to peer through the smoke he was even more surprised at what he saw. Lying on the ground with his head raised was a large golden lion. He looked at Little Ed with large eyes which were both soft and strong.

"Are you my new solar plexus animal?" asked Little Ed incredulously.

"I am," answered the lion in his deeply settled voice.

"I don't understand what happened to the raccoon," said Little Ed.

"His abilities are still within me," answered the lion, "but there is now much more as well. In order to fully act, you must also be able to fully relax, and I am a master at both."

The other animals crowded around Lion, admiring, commenting on his fine mane, appreciating this transformation. Little Ed knew that what they were appreciating was truly valuable, and he vowed silently that he would walk the path of transformation as fully as possible.

Discovering Himself

In the days and weeks that followed, Little Ed felt himself to be different in ways that were difficult for him to describe. There was a persistent quality of stillness that he had not experienced before, and even though he tried to discover its location it seemed to pervade the entire space in which he found himself. It wasn't a feeling so much as a kind of awareness that permeated the surrounding space, and although the particular events in his life didn't seem to have changed, his way of being with them had, and this itself made him more available to them and at the same time free from them. Instead of being tied to a predictable response, he felt freer to play with the events, and many times they took on a humorous quality.

Little Ed found that he could be with a situation for a much longer time before he needed to act, and that his actions were not as compulsive as they had been, but now seemed impelled from within, as if the possibilities of action were much broader, and something within him chose the appropriate act related to the specific situation, rather than having a single response for a general class of events. There seemed to be no rules for what he did. No, that was not it. What he did came not from a series of rules he had learned intellectually, but seemed to evolve naturally out of taking in all of what was going on, with a tremendous quality of finesse, so that his actions became much more fluid and precisely related to the surrounding events.

And he found himself being naturally orderly, replacing tools exactly where he had gotten them and even remembering the exact design of the grain on the handle, for example. And this without thinking about it. As if, yes, this belongs exactly here, this is its home, where it is comfortable, and in appropriate relationship with all the other tools and the people who use them. And he found himself talking tenderly to the tools, saying hello to them when he first approached them, thanking each tool after he had used it, appreciating a particularly skillful cut that the tool had made, feeling the tool, hefting it in his hand, appreciating its weight and temperature, and the wood and metal from which it was made. It was as if a growing intimacy was taking place with everything that he came in contact with, a familiarity, a new found family. Everything that surrounded him was now his family.

But most of all, he was aware that his relationship with Golden Bear had changed significantly. Even though little was said between them, there seemed no need to converse. Little Ed was much more alert to the subtlety of Golden Bear's actions. He would call Little Ed over with a slight movement of his head, or ask for a tool by moving a finger and Little Ed knew immediately which tool he wanted. He seemed to be more finely attuned to what Golden Bear was aware of, but without losing his own awareness. In fact, it seemed to be a natural outgrowth of his own greater awareness. It seemed his own awareness had grown to the point of including other awarenesses and knowing them in certain ways.

But the most profound thing was how he felt about himself. He was at home in himself, aware of a funny side of himself, appreciative of the ongoing discovery of who he was, sensitive to a particular aliveness that was always on the edge of things and events. In fact all things seemed to be events in themselves. The set of tools was no longer a group of objects but a number of unique, ongoing personalities with which he carried on an alive relationship and he was aware of himself in that relationship, feeling that the tool also was aware of him. He was also an ongoing event along with the myriad of other ongoing events that were constantly taking place. But the events took place within the stillness which he had become.

He found that he was no longer stern with himself but much more allowing, and what would have been an error or a mistake in the past was now an occurrence that had a humorous side. And sometimes the error, if he followed it closely, would lead him to a new discovery, to seeing a new way of doing something, a new way of using the tool or of approaching the grain of the wood. Mistakes now seemed to be doorways opening to unknown places, invitations to explore new dimensions which had been hidden beneath the "right" way of doing things. His life had become a constant, ongoing adventure.

There was a subtle joy in his being alive. In the morning he would awaken with a sense of excitement and curiosity. And the first thing he would do would be to greet his animals (including the tree and the sunshine, of course). Nothing extensive, he would just travel to them and say hello and ask if they needed anything. Or, he might ask them to comment on a particular carving he was about to undertake. Usually they would just tell him to enjoy it but sometimes they would comment specifically, suggesting that he begin with a particular part of the design, or pointing out a particular turn to the grain in the wood. Frequently they were just funny. The tree said one day about a particular piece of wood that Little Ed was going to carve, "This looks like my cousin!" at which all of the animals and Little Ed laughed. Little Ed felt their support and also their ease and freedom. And he felt a deep love for them all just exactly as they were.

The Golden Bear

Little Ed didn't know how much time had passed. In fact, time itself had ceased to be a thing and was more like a sea of events which had their own currents and eddies: moving, evolving, changing. He was aware that his skill had grown significantly, and he now worked easily along with Golden Bear, as if they were two hands working on the same project. At times they would stop and appreciate each other's work, or the work in general, or make a comment on a particularly difficult cut, or ask each other's advice, or just laugh together.

Ever since he had met his own animals Little Ed had been curious about the animals of others. He found himself sometimes wondering what his sister's animals were, or his mother's, or his father's. But most of all he was curious about Golden Bear's animals. Once he had even asked his own animals if they knew what Golden Bear's animals were. Their reply was not direct but there was an implication that they knew Golden Bear's animals personally; what they said was that if it were appropriate, Golden Bear himself would tell him. And they pointed out to Little Ed the interface between curiosity and stillness, and how if these could both be maintained together the opening itself would come in its own time.

One day, as they were nearing completion of the work on the pole, Golden Bear remarked that the organization that had commissioned the pole had previously been quite opposed to craftsmanship as a way of life.

"There was a time when anything that did not come from thinking was looked down upon as not having quite the same value as those things that stemmed from the intellect. But that was a time when people were very divided within themselves. The original division was within each person, and that then came to be expressed by people dividing themselves into groups against one another. I belonged to one of those groups myself."

Little Ed's ears opened wide and he could feel the rabbit sniffing the air. Golden Bear was a man who did not often talk about his past, so this was a real treat and Little Ed waited expectantly for him to go on.

In a monologue that was equally reminiscent and instructive, Golden Bear continued. "My skill, like yours, has always been in my hands. They have an intelligence and a way of knowing that is much more skillful than my thinking. I used to carve small pieces of fossilized ivory. It was something my grandfather had shown me how to do. I always had a piece in my pocket that I was working on. There was something about feeling it in my pocket, knowing it was there, that was comforting to me. Especially in the school I was forced to attend."

Little Ed was frozen in attentive stillness. He could feel all of his animals alert. Golden Bear had never spoken of "school" before. Little Ed waited with both horror and anticipation, because from what he knew of "school," there had been nothing more stifling and deadening.

"The teacher was a large man who was quite mean and limited. I see now how he was trapped and frozen in his thinking, and I feel sorry for him, but he should never have been allowed to impose himself on children.

"At that time, what was required of me was to learn a foreign language: English. It was very different from the way I thought and the teacher acted as if there was something wrong with my own way of thinking. As best as I could guess, he felt that all people should have the same thoughts and come to thinking in the same way. This felt to me like there was no room for who I was.

"His way of 'teaching' was to have a student stand and read words out of a book. Of course all the other students were happy it was not them having to do it, but everyone had to at some time. After the student had read, the teacher would then pick out all of the mistakes he had made and tell the class what they were. I always felt humiliated by this, but I see now that is exactly what he wanted to do and that he used his teaching in order to accomplish it; he was a man who felt very humiliated at not being whole and he hid it by inflicting his humiliation on others.

"On one particular occasion he had me read a long passage from a book. I felt I had done it particularly well but he seemed to call up mistakes almost out of nowhere. When he had finished pointing out the mistakes he then began commenting on how I was dressed and talking about the poverty I came from and how only through schooling could I hope to become someone.

"There was a part of me, deep inside, that rebelled at hearing this, and swore that he would never separate me from who I was. After this I became very silent and spoke to no one. In school I would do the bare minimum, and speak only when it was absolutely essential. Whenever I had to read I would have a separate voice going inside me, swearing that I would never give in to becoming the machine he was trying to turn me into, while on the surface I was reading obediently.

"Over time I became deeply divided within myself.

Outwardly I would conform readily to whatever was required of me, but deep within I was against all teachers and all schools and all authority.

"My only solace, the only place where I felt whole, was when I was carving. I had a favorite spot that I would go to whenever I could. It was up on a small hill in an excavation between some large boulders. There I would take out my ivory from the leather pouch in which I always carried it and I would work on the carving. I always carved animal figures in the style I had learned from my grandfather.

"I was carving a bear, and no matter how hard I tried to make it different, the bears eyes always looked very sad, as if he were in agony. I worked long and tediously around those eyes, feeling that if only I could get it right the bear's eyes would be strong and stern, but it seemed the more I worked on it the sadder the eyes became."

Little Ed reminisced about how he had been taught by Golden Bear to allow the animal to emerge on its own from the wood, to allow the animal itself to use Little Ed's hands and tools in order to come forth out of the wood, as if this were its means of being born, and that the birthing was a natural process that happened in its own way when the time was right.

"The eyes were always very important in the way of carving I had learned. I finally realized that I couldn't make the eyes any different than they were and so I went on to carving the rest of the bear. For some reason I left its belly until last and whenever I would come to carving the belly I would think of my teacher and of how I hated him. I had difficulty with the belly and I finally realized that there was another animal there, a very angry animal that had its teeth buried in the bear's belly. By now I was just letting my hands carve, without trying to change what they were doing.

"In school it seemed that the more silent I became the more the teacher found to fault me with, and I began feeling that he relished having me read so he could criticize me. About that time I also got the idea to burn the school down, so one evening when I found it difficult to work on my bear I took some rags that I had been saving and soaked them in gasoline. I put them under the stairway inside the school and set them on fire."

Little Ed listened with rapt attention. He did not think it possible that Golden Bear could do the things he heard him describing.

"Fortunately, the fire was extinguished before it ignited the entire building," continued Golden Bear with a chuckle, "and only a few stairs were burned. Of course, I was accused and sent to prison. The teacher testified against me. I said absolutely nothing during the entire hearing.

"This was the best thing that could have happened to me. In prison I met an old Indian who knew about the inner animals. At that time the animals were known to very few, but he was one of them.

"One day he saw me carving my ivory. I was working on it with the needle that had been given me in the prison for stitching my clothes. He was intensely curious about it and he asked me where those animals lived. I thought he was a little crazy for asking this; obviously the bear lives in the forest and the sea monster that was biting his belly lives in the sea. The old man just looked at me for a long time and then said, very seriously, 'No, I mean where do they live in you?'

"I didn't know what to think. I must have looked at him as if he were completely crazy. And at the same time something in me knew what he was asking. I went into what felt like a dream and I could see that the bear with the very sad eyes was in my heart and that the sea monster was in my solar plexus, reaching up and biting the bear's belly.

"The old man asked me to talk to them. I felt I didn't know what I was doing, all of this was so strange and different. But I asked the sea monster why he was biting the bear's belly and he told me that it was in order to get my attention. I was surprised to hear this and I asked him why he needed my attention. He answered, 'So that you can begin to come back home to yourself!'

"When I heard this I began to cry. I felt ashamed of my crying but the old man just held me and encouraged me to allow myself to cry. As I cried I could see the sea monster opening its jaws and releasing the bear. The bear let out a sigh of relief and its eyes began to change. The bear itself began to glow with a golden light.

"I knew then that I had found a real teacher even if I had to come to prison to find him."

Freedom and Slavery

Little Ed was struck by how intimately connected Golden Bear's knowledge of the animals was with his vocation as a woodcarver. As if his animals had used his carving as a means for coming forth so they could help him grow. And the more he came to know of Golden Bear the more he held him in respect.

"I was in prison for three years," Golden Bear continued. "It was lucky I met the old Indian when I first went in. I spent all the time I could with him. He knew things about me that I never knew myself, yet I see now that they must have been obvious at the time. He became the best friend I had ever had, I could talk to him about anything. He saw me groping for my path in the dark and helped shine some light where it would help me see. I have always felt that I went to prison in order to meet him. I don't know that my windows of feeling and imagery would ever have been opened had it not been for him.

"He made me aware that I had lived most of my life in hate and anger and, curiously, he didn't condemn me for that. I say curiously because up until that time all authorities had told me that anger was bad. He said I had spent my life developing a certain kind of power and that now it was time for that power to become fuel for my growing. I was afraid initially, because I felt that if that anger fueled my growing I would be totally and relentlessly angry. He told me that my thinking was mistaken and that my thinking didn't yet know about the sources of fuel for growing, since my thinking didn't yet know much about growing.

"He taught me that my thinking felt it had to protect the knowing it already had, and rightfully so, but that it was also hungry for new knowledge, and that it had to open to the new knowledge at its own pace, and that my job was to help it experience the fear and wariness of opening to new knowledge. He helped me begin to have a relationship with my fear by showing me where it came from. He also helped me see that my fear was really the excitement of new awareness but in a tremendously compressed state. That is why patience and persistence were so essential to help it decompress. It was like a very volatile fuel which if ignited all at once would just explode, but if it could be meted out at a measured pace it could fuel a tremendous amount of growing. He told me that most people waste the fuel that is available to their growing because they don't know what it is.

"He also made sure I understood that growing is always positive. He said a plant always grows toward the light; that is the only way it can grow, and that it must grow at its own pace. Growing cannot be demanded of it, but only nurtured and supported. He helped me shift my orientation from learning, which I had come to hate as a result of the cruel teacher I had, to growing, which was always positive and which he said was essentially the ongoing discovery of who I truly am."

Little Ed was drinking in every word that Golden Bear spoke.

"The old Indian had never been to school, but he had learned much about it from people who had, and he said that for all he could understand, much of school had nothing to do with learning, but seemed to have to do with controlling and subordinating people. Of course this was before the time of the great Shipshift.

"That was the shift from ownership to relationship, but what did it have to do with school?" asked Little Ed.

"Before this time, many parents held the attitude that they owned their children, rather than realizing that children were in need of relationship. In owning their children they felt that they could determine them completely; they had no trust in children growing the way they needed to. Growing requires the relationship of trust and in ownership there is no place for trust, only control. So schools had become an extension of that attitude: children 'belonged' to certain schools and the adults that they became constantly needed something to 'belong to.' So that people came to feel secure only if they were owned in some way: by an organization, by an idea, by an ideology. Eventually they came to be owned by their own thinking. They didn't realize that this ownership was a form of slavery. Freedom cannot exist in slavery, only in full relationship. So it was the development of a relationship with thinking that had the most to do with freeing children from being owned by parents, schools and teachers.

"Thinking is usually focused on what is being thought about but growing involves coming to the origin of the thinking in its relationship with all the other aspects of who we are.

"The old Indian not only introduced me to parts of myself that I had never met before, but he was available to help me develop a relationship with them. And it was in the fullness of that relationship that I came to find my own freedom, even though I was in prison."

Identity

"One day the old Indian gave me a piece of deer antler and suggested I carve my animals on it in the order that they lived in my body. I was diligently into the carving before I realized that I was carving a small totem pole. When I told him of my discovery, he said that totem poles had been the way our ancestors had of displaying their power. It was a way of putting on display the intimacy of who one really is and of supporting that for all to see. In this way one does not get caught up in an identity separate from relationship."

"The totem pole has always been a mystery to me," replied Little Ed, "and I understand it better now from what you have said, but I don't know what you mean about identity."

"Identity is separate from who one is," explained Golden Bear. "At its best it is thinking's attempt to describe the mystery of who one is in one's ongoing awareness. But thinking is always a pace behind, trying to catch up; its frustration is that it never can. When thinking understands this, then it can relax and have fun with what it is capable of doing, rather than being obsessed with getting it 'right.'

Thinking has been taught that it is essential to who we are, but that is just not true. In the maintenance of this belief, thinking is perhaps most intrusive into who we really are. Thinking maintains its hold by grabbing our awareness, just as it grabbed your awareness through the thought of killing your little sister."

"But I never would let myself think of that except for the time that it first occurred," answered Little Ed in some agitation.

"Exactly!" said Golden Bear. "Thinking gained even more power, by becoming that which would protect you from itself. Thinking became the rescuer that protected you from your fear of thinking."

Little Ed felt himself beginning to become confused, and he told Golden Bear about it.

"Stay with yourself even through this confusion," he advised Little Ed. "Confusion is one of thinking's ways of protecting its old patterns. Let yourself feel the discomfort that accompanies the confusion, talk to that discomfort, ask it to help you grow."

Little Ed did this and soon came to a place of stillness and clarity.

"Rather than allowing our thinking to evolve naturally and organically, people had become obsessed with forming it into certain structures. Since these structures are formed by people deliberately, they became the social forms within which our thinking felt it must live in order to survive.

"One of these structures is a description of who we are. We might think that the description is purely factual, but it is actually concerned as much with what it leaves out as with what it includes. You would never have described yourself as a four-year old murderer, would you?"

"Definitely not!" replied Little Ed.

"Requiring these descriptions at the times they occur, although seemingly innocent enough, imposes the demand that we protect ourselves. When a child is asked, 'What are you doing? Why did you do that? What are you going to do?' there is the unspoken demand that the answer conform to the expectations of the questioner, and the child, brilliant being that he is, learns to supply what is asked for. This is the beginning of a way of describing ourselves that will be sanctioned by society. It is also the beginning of a crystallized identity, for we soon begin to think that we have to conform to the description.

"Thus thinking begins to believe that it is essential in order for us to be who we are. It is not, of course. But it is essential in order for us to continue to maintain the description that we think others want to hear. However, doing this is at odds with our own wholeness. It is this division in our wholeness that is so destructive. And in order for our wholeness to return, thinking must return to its proper relationship with the other dimensions of who we are. In order for thinking to do this we must give up that identity we maintain for the other person to see and become once again the ongoing experience that we truly are. Then we have room to grow."

The Totem Pole

By now, Little Ed was fully aware of his own rhythm in carving, and that the rhythm varied and changed depending on the grain of the wood, the sharpness of the tool, and the quality of detail involved in the carving. The pole on which they had been working was nearing completion, and although Little Ed had been responsible for only a small portion of it he felt as proud as if he had carved the entire thing. He had also become deeply respectful of the way Golden Bear would talk to the pole, would greet it in the morning, speaking to it gently and lovingly, and would invite the particular animal he was working on to show itself strongly, to help him with certain difficult aspects of its carving, and then thank it for its help.

When it was finally complete, Golden Bear went into the village to invite the people to come help him transport it from the carving shed to the dock where it could be loaded onto the boat. The pole was not a large one and the twelve people who came carried it easily. Three small carrying poles were slipped under it. Two people on each side of the totem pole grasped the end of each carrying pole. Golden Bear had put on a beautiful black cape which bore the design of a red eagle outlined in buttons made of mother-of-pearl. He carried a special drum which he beat in an accelerating rhythm. The drumbeat suddenly stopped and the people raised the totem pole. Golden Bear, Anora, and Little Ed then accompanied the pole bearers as far as the boat.

"This pole will stand in the lobby of a bank," said Golden Bear to Little Ed, "so here we must say goodbye to it. In other times we might have accompanied it to its final home and held a celebration for it at that place."

In sadness they each said goodbye to it. Little Ed thanked it for having taught him so much and wished it well in its new home, thinking fleetingly of his own Ceremony of Severance.

As the days passed, Little Ed began to become aware of something forming within himself. His mind and thinking seemed to be in a state of flux, but within this a development was taking place which felt like the formation of an embryo, each day taking on more definite form and configuration. Then one day the realization came.

"I want to carve a totem pole . . . my totem pole," he said to Golden Bear.

Golden Bear stopped what he was doing and looked deeply at Little Ed, deeper than Little Ed had ever felt him look before, as if he were looking at something within but beyond who Little Ed was.

"Yes. It is time."

Little Ed felt a shiver run through him as Golden Bear said these words.

Although Little Ed had expected to carve a small totem pole he was surprised when Golden Bear began telling him about the sacred way to call a tree.

"Carving your totem pole is a sacred task, and you must be particularly respectful at every step along the way," said Golden Bear. "First, you must go visit your animals with a specific intent: that intent is to ask their permission to carve the pole and to invite their participation. Without their permission and participation you don't have a chance.

"Next, you must call the tree. This doesn't mean that you go outside and yell for a tree," said Golden Bear with a chuckle, "but that you invite your animals to help you know how to select the proper tree. They may take you on a journey and actually show you the tree, or they may just talk to you, telling you about its properties. Once the tree has been called, then you must go find it in the woods. When you find it, make it an offering of something that you prize and then ask its permission to enter into the spirit of your totem animals. If it agrees, then you can begin to fell it.

"Some people prefer to spend some time talking to the tree, asking it to tell them about itself and drinking of its wisdom. This could go on for months before they finally fell it. I don't care for that approach myself. To me it feels somewhat diversionary, and besides, there is always a sadness when you finally fell it."

Little Ed began to feel the seriousness of what he was undertaking, and he didn't know if he would have the heart to fell a living tree in order to carve a totem pole. After all, one of his own animals was a tree!

Golden Bear had Little Ed sit in his large comfortable chair while he went to visit his animals. When he approached them in the beautiful sunshine-filled valley where they lived, he could see that they were serious, perhaps even solemn. They were all gathered under his forehead tree. The bird was on the low branch where he typically perched when they met in council. The golden lion was comfortably resting on the eastern edge of the circle and the flying white horse stood nobly at the west. The rabbit and the bear cub were the first to greet Little Ed. Golden sunshine filled and surrounded the circle of animals.

After greeting them, he told them that he had been having thoughts about carving a totem pole and he asked if it would be okay with them. They all looked at him earnestly, and one by one nodded their assent. He then asked if they would help with the carving. At this they felt a need to huddle together. Little Ed didn't know what they were discussing, but they finally turned and addressed him.

"We will help you if you will lead us," said the golden lion.

Little Ed felt a sudden strange panic upon hearing these words. His first thought was to run away from the animals and to go back home to his mother and father. He realized how extreme this thought was, and he knew that something was happening here that he didn't understand, but by now he had come to learn to trust events like this. He knew that in some way his growing would be involved.

"I feel a sudden panic when I hear you say that, Lion, and I feel like running away and going back home to my parents," he said.

The other animals laughed and said, "Then we won't

elect you president."

These words plunged into Little Ed's memory, taking him back to a long forgotten event. It was one of the group meetings that were regularly held with other children who were in his Developmental Expression program. He was eight years old. The children were being introduced to styles of government and as part of the experience they were to hold an election. Little Ed had been nominated for president and was asked to give a speech on why the others should vote for him. He felt that to be president was an awesome responsibility and he had no idea how to go about it. He felt overwhelmed and as time drew closer for him to deliver his speech, he began to feel a real panic and just wanted to leave and go home. When it was finally time for him to give the speech he found himself able to say only a few words and he was trembling the entire time. He was extremely uncomfortable and felt deeply humiliated by this experience.

When Little Ed returned from this memory to the council of animals, he noticed that the rabbit was trembling. The other animals were just looking at the rabbit. "I don't know what's wrong," the rabbit said, "but I feel terrified."

"I know just how you feel," said Little Ed, "but I don't know why you feel that way."

"Hold me," said the rabbit, "please hold me. I'm scared."

Little Ed embraced the rabbit and realized that it was much larger than when he had first met it. "I didn't know you had grown so," he said.

"Yes," replied the rabbit, "I had to grow big enough to face my fears."

As Little Ed held the rabbit he felt his own fear well up within himself. In a strange way he felt himself embracing his fear in the same way he was embracing the rabbit. There was no attempt to get rid of the fear, or to run away from it, in fact, he actually felt some compassion for the fear. In embracing it he began to feel its contours and the subtlety of its edges. He saw it as a living organic energy whose edges were so sensitive that most experiences were too much for it and it would recoil at the slightest unexpected movement. Eventually the fear relaxed and became warm and Little Ed suddenly realized he was still holding the warm rabbit.

Only something was different! The rabbit was purring. Surprised at this he looked more closely only to be totally shocked that he was now holding a cat that was sound asleep and purring. He held it gently, feeling the strong purr penetrating his own body, down into the marrow of his bones, a profound vibration.

The animals gathered around to look at the cat and as they did so it began to awaken, stretching its limbs, yawning, and extending its claws. Little Ed was surprised to see how large and sharp the claws were. The cat then turned its head and looked Little Ed squarely in the face. His head jerked back abruptly as he realized that this was not a housecat as he had supposed, but a small mountain lion.

Little Ed looked at the other animals and was surprised to hear himself say to them, "Now I can lead you."

They replied as one: "Now there is no need for you to!"

Calling The Tree

The animals took Little Ed on a long journey, through the woods and over hills. They came to a narrow stream that looked strangely familiar. As they looked across it they could see a circular clearing in the center of which stood a tall straight cedar. Little Ed knew immediately that this would be his totem pole.

They all crossed the stream in a rush of excitement. Then the animals held back as Little Ed walked slowly up to the tree.

"Honored tree," he said, "I wish to offer you this gift of my own water." With that, he urinated at the base of the tree. Little Ed himself was surprised at this strange offering.

"Thank you for your water," replied the tree when Little Ed had finished urinating.

"I didn't mean to offend you," answered Little Ed hastily.

"I am not in the least offended," answered the tree, "on the contrary, I am deeply grateful."

Little Ed could feel something tugging at his mind, as if something were changing at a very deep level, but he could not give it any articulation in words at this point.

"Fine straight cedar," Little Ed continued, addressing the tree somewhat formally, "I come to ask if you would allow your spirit to enter into my animals in the form of a totem pole. I would have to fell you, and I feel sadness at having to do that, but I would always treat you with great honor and respect."

"My friend," answered the tree, "I am but one of many, many who have stood anchored on this earth, and we have always given ourselves freely to the needs of those who move about. We have been shelter and food, we have been tools and weapons, we have been clothing and fuel, we have been fine creations and we have been trash for them. Even so, they have never fully understood us.

"Being anchored in one place, drinking directly of the soil, standing nakedly through all the seasons, growing to great ages, we have seen and learned things that few of those who move about will ever have the opportunity to know. We know eternity directly and we are completely open to the transformations that occur. I would be honored to meet your animals at that place where they could feel my age and anchorage and I could feel their individuality and relationship.

"Furthermore," continued the tree, "most of my roots have already begun to cease drinking from the soil and the juices move more and more slowly up into my branches. I have begun to dry and become rigid. So you come at the best possible time for me. I will gladly lend my essence to your animals.

"But there is one thing I ask of you: whenever you meet my brothers in your life, treat them with dignity and respect, for we are your very ancient relatives."

Little Ed felt chilled by this final statement. Even though his forehead animal was a tree, he had never really thought of himself as perhaps having evolved from a tree, and he was suddenly beginning to feel that not only he evolved from plants, but that his life and the lives of all his ancestors had always been intimately involved with trees. This was an ongoing living relationship of which he had been generally oblivious, but now it seemed so blatantly obvious. And certainly the wood that he loved to carve all came from trees.

He felt a deep sense of gratitude toward this tree and toward all trees, and he knew now of the unselfish caring that the trees felt for all the rest of life. It was with deep feeling that he now addressed the tree.

"Thank you, Great Tree. The totem pole to which you give yourself so graciously will always remind me of the essential relationship between the beings who are anchored in the earth and the beings who move about, and I vow to treat you and your brothers with deep respect."

The Event

Little Ed and Golden Bear set out into the forest the very next morning to seek the tree that the animals had shown him. They ate a hearty breakfast which Anora had prepared and took a small bag of bread and fruit, and a container of water. Little Ed noticed that Golden Bear seemed to take a particularly long time to say goodbye to Anora and to hold her before they left.

Little Ed was jubilant as he walked through the forest. His body felt light with an energy that bubbled forth spontaneously and playfully. He breathed the fresh, crisp air in large, full gulps and his senses were particularly keen. Birds sang in the trees, small animals scurried about at their aproach and there was a fullness in the forest that Little Ed had never felt before.

Little Ed carried the axe with which he would fell the tree and Golden Bear carried a coil of rope over his shoulder from which they would fashion a harness for carrying the tree back to the shop if it weren't too heavy; otherwise they would have to bring more help.

Although they were travelling together, Little Ed felt

that Golden Bear was very deliberate about the directions they took, as if he already knew where the tree would be found. As these thoughts were running through his mind, they came upon a stream that seemed familiar. Could it be the same stream the animals had taken him across?

As they looked for a convenient place to cross the stream, Little Ed looked across it and was stunned to see a circular clearing. In the center of it stood the tall straight cedar.

Paying no heed to the water, Little Ed rushed across the stream and up to the tree. As he approached he suddenly remembered something. Taking the container of water they had brought, Little Ed uncapped it and poured some at the base of the tree. "Fine tree, I bring you an offering of water," he said.

The tree remained silent.

"I thank you for offering yourself to me for the carving of my totem pole and for all you taught me when my animals first brought you to me."

Still the tree was silent.

Without delay, Little Ed raised the axe and began

cutting the tree. Golden Bear waited at a respectful distance.

Little Ed was consumed by his energy and flailed intensely with the axe. Chips flew and the tree began to creak. At a solid thrust the tree shifted slightly and wedged the axe tightly within the cut. Little Ed pushed and strained but the axe would not budge. He moved around to the other side and pulled on the handle with all his might, but still it held fast. Golden Bear was moving forward to give him a hand when suddenly the tree shifted a bit more and began to topple. Golden Bear rushed to grab Little Ed out of its path and just as he reached the tree he slipped on the wet spot where Little Ed had made his offering. With one great lunge he pushed Little Ed out of the path of the falling tree but was himself caught beneath it.

Spitting the dirt out of his mouth, Little Ed gathered himself up from the place where he fell and rushed over to Golden Bear. The tree had fallen directly cross his chest and crushed it. He did not move. Little Ed grabbed the trunk of the tree and heaved with all his might. The tree, weighted more by its branches, shifted and the trunk swung off Golden Bear. He lay completely still. Little Ed crumpled over him, frantically searching for a heartbeat, for a sign of breathing, for a pulse. There was none.

Little Ed held him closely as his own body heaved

and rocked with great sobs that came from the depths of his being. The woods were intensely still. In the circular clearing, with the felled tree, the boy held his dear friend and rocked and rocked and rocked.

The Passageway

The days that followed were a general dark blur. Little Ed could not believe what had happened, nor that it had happened so suddenly and unexpectedly. His sadness and anguish were overwhelming.

At first, he racked his memory to see what he might have done differently: if only he had not poured the water, Golden Bear would not have slipped, if only he had not rushed in so immediately to cut the tree, the axe would not have gotten stuck, if only he had taken the tree's silence as an indication not to cut it, if only he had not gotten the idea in the first place to carve a totem pole, and on and on and on. When his thinking was at the point of exhaustion trying to come up with reasons why or with ways that would have allowed a different outcome, Little Ed's own forehead tree suddenly appeared to him.

"You cannot undo the events by thinking," it said. "There is no way that you can undo what has been done, even though you are willing to take full responsibility for it. Rather than straining your thinking and driving yourelf crazy by trying to figure out a way for this not to have happened, you must ask your thinking to support you in the experiences that are now necessary. There is nothing your thinking needs to do at this time other than to support you fully in your feeling. This is a time for the boundaries of feeling to stretch and grow. It is a time for you to feel as fully as you possibly can, with no holding back. In fact, you must be willing to step forth voluntarily into the feelings that are making themselves known to you. The death of Golden Bear is a powerful event for your growing. Don't dishonor him by wasting it in regret. Accept it fully and allow yourself to traverse this passageway completely."

Little Ed was stunned to hear his tree say this and he became aware of how automatically he had been trying to avoid the truth of the situation. Golden Bear was dead! However it had come about, through whatever conjunction of circumstances and events, it was now unavoidable that Golden Bear was dead. No thinking, no doing on his part, could undo this fact. Golden Bear was dead. He suddenly remembered the vow that he had silently made upon the transformation of the raccoon into the golden lion. His path would be the path of transformation.

Little Ed called upon all his animals and the tree and the sunshine to come be with him during this time. He asked them to support him for whatever needed to happen, and to help him face directly any and all of the experiences that presented themselves. He asked them to hold him during this time and to help him feel as fully as possible all feelings, no matter how intense. And he invited his energy in general to grow him as fully as it possibly could.

The animals did just that. He could feel their presence as he remembered the first time he had ever seen Golden Bear, and the strange feeling he had experienced in his heart and solar plexus. Upon remembering this he burst into tears and fell on the floor, great sobs heaving his body. He allowed it to move however it moved, without trying to interfere, just allowing himself to be fully present. Finally the sobbing stopped and his body lay still.

Anora

Little Ed remembered how he had rushed to the cabin, feeling the dread of what he had to tell Anora. He was surprised to see her waiting at the edge of the path that led from their home. He fell into her open arms, tear-stained and dusty. She held and rocked him as he cried and cried. Little Ed felt her sadness, and knew that she had known what he was coming to tell her.

Together they returned to the clearing and using the rope Golden Bear himself had brought, they tied his hands and feet to a long narrow pole and carried him back to the house.

Anora's presence filled the house as she washed Golden Bear's body and dressed him in clean white clothes, laying him out on the bed.

Little Ed seemed to notice for the first time, although he had seen them many times before, the numerous herbs and roots and stems that were bundled together, hanging in small clusters from the ceiling. He understood that Anora had gathered these, and that she had a deep knowing about the small things that grew in the forest and their uses. She had crumbled some of these into the water which she had used for the washing. Little Ed saw a brightness around Anora that he had never seen before.

"I will spend the night watching over the body," she said to Little Ed, "and there are things you must do and things I will tell you."

Little Ed was surprised at the firmness and solidness in her voice.

"First, I must tell you of the dream this beautiful bear has had three times. It was of a great totem pole, the largest he had ever seen. He was awed by its height and its girth. He had never seen a tree large enough for the carving of such a pole. It towered above the forests and the mountains and it reached so high into the sky that he could not see where it ended. As he stood there, not knowing what to make of such a grand pole, a bird arrived, a raven, and it flew down and stood on his shoulder.

"As he always did whenever he met an animal, he greeted it and asked if it had come for a reason. 'I am to take you to the top of this pole,' said the raven. 'Are you ready to come with me?'

"This beautiful bear told me that he knew this was

no ordinary invitation, and that if he went with the raven he might never return. He glanced at the great pole that rose into the sky and as he did so he recognized that some of the animals carved into it were his own. He particularly recognized the golden bear of his heart, the one that gave him his own name. He knew then what an honor the raven had been extending him with its invitation, and without hestiation he climbed onto the raven's back for the flight.

"The raven flew higher and higher until they were so high that the beautiful bear could no longer see the earth below, and still the pole extended up beyond his ability to see its top. As they rose higher and higher he realized that they were heading toward the sun, and that the pole seemed to have its origin in the sun.

"As they reached the sun the raven flew directly into it and the beautiful bear felt himself transformed into the rays of the sun, and he himself then shone down onto everything in one continuous stream. He told me he could feel himself present in everything below, and that he was now the glow of the world and everything in it.

"Last night he had the dream for the third time.

"Now you must go into the village and tell them what has happened. You need not tell everyone. They will all know quickly anyway. Tell them I will stay with him tonight and they must come in the morning."

The Gathering

People began arriving with the dawn and they immediately set to work. The men gathered wood and built a large fire and the women began to prepare a meal out of food they had brought with them. There were warm words of greeting and acknowledgement and everyone seemed to know exactly what to do. Some of the men brought tools and carried them to a distant hill where they set about building a platform higher than a man's head.

Everyone greeted Little Ed warmly, including many people he had never met, yet they all seemed to know him. He had dressed in the best clothes he had and he set to work with the men.

After the platform was built, they all returned to the house. The meal was now ready and Anora emerged from the house. Little Ed knew that Anora had not slept, and yet she looked brilliantly alert. Everyone rushed up to hug her and hold her. There was a radiance about her. She also held everyone and radiated warmly upon them. Little Ed remembered suddenly about the dream.

Then an old, old man arrived. His hair was snowy

white, braided into a thick single braid wrapped with a red cloth. He was bent, yet he seemd to move like a cat. Little Ed had never seen anyone older than him. All greeted him warmly. When Little Ed greeted him he looked at Little Ed as if he had always known him.

They all shared the meal, chatting animatedly and telling things that they remembered about Golden Bear. Little Ed was surprised at how many of these stories were humorous.

Following the meal, several men entered the house and emerged carrying the body of Golden Bear lying on one of the doors that had been removed from its hinges. Anora had dressed him in all his finery: a red headband on his brow, a beaded pendant around his neck, his finest moccasins, and his belt with the silver buckle. He looked radiant.

Silently they carried him to the platform on the hill, everyone trailing behind like a long snake. His body was placed on the platform and the old, old man spoke. Little Ed was surprised at how strong his voice was.

"My old friend who came forth from this universe many years ago has now returned to rejoin it once again. But even as I speak that, I know it is not true, because my friend never left the universe, he lived in it fully and was guided by it throughout his life. And just as he shared himself with so many while he walked in this body, now he offers this body to any that may have need of it: the animals, the sky, the wind and rain, the earth, the plants, the trees."

With this the old, old man took a small leather pouch from his belt and opened it. He withdrew something small and brownish-white that he placed next to Golden Bear's body on the platform. Little Ed strained to see what it was. All he could see was that it was a small carving of an animal whose eyes were very, very sad.

The Flow

The next morning when he awoke he suddenly remembered that Golden Bear was no longer alive and a deep moaning issued forth from his chest. He felt himself embracing the moaning the way he had once embraced the rabbit and his fear, and he held it and rocked back and forth as if he were holding a small child.

Upon entering the shop for the first time since Golden Bear died, he suddenly became angry at all the tools and at woodcarving itself. He let himself feel this fully, aware that the flying white horse and the golden lion were close by at his sides. Eventually the anger subsided and a deep sadness ensued. He embraced the sadness as well, telling it that it could have all the space within himself that it needed, that he would not chase it away. At this a deep feeling of warmth enveloped him and he sat in Golden Bear's large comfortable chair.

Thoughts of the many different conversations they had had, of the warmth they felt for each other, of the small events that transpired in their relationship flowed easily through Little Ed's mind, and the feelings of those incidents, as well as the sadness at Golden Bear's absence, became like rivers, moving swiftly here, coming to a soft broad flow there, narrowing into a fast, rock-cutting intensity, seeping into the earth, and ultimately coming to that timeless sea of endless age and depth.

Allowing the fullness of his experience became Little Ed's primary focus and he felt there was nothing more important at this time than to let himself step fully into each experience as it presented itself, with all of its memories and thoughts, all of its feelings, all of its reflections upon the moment, right here, right now. To someone observing him he might have appeared to be in a slight daze, perhaps somewhat inattentive, or as someone whose focus was on a dimension that others could not see.

As the days passed, Little Ed found himself feeling stronger and stronger, completely available to the flow of the present moment, deeply centered in a way he had never been before. His actions were forceful and deliberate. He felt solid and capable, and although his friend was dead, there was a way in which they were very much together.

Wolf

One day his bear cub came to him and Little Ed was surprised to see that he was quite sad.

"You look so sad," said Little Ed.

"You need to come with me," said the bear cub and it began moving immediately from its blackberry patch up into the hills. Little Ed followed at a fast pace, wondering where it could be taking him and why it was so sad; after all, he no longer was. They travelled for a considerable distance until they finally reached a high ledge. When they stopped Little Ed saw that there was a wolf on the ledge. The wolf had its head raised, howling. Little Ed had never seen this wolf before.

Little Ed asked the bear cub why he had brought him here. "Ask the wolf," answered the cub.

Little Ed asked the wolf, "Why was I brought here?"

The wolf answered, "Come howl with me!"

At this Little Ed noticed that the wolf was standing

over the very spot where Golden Bear had died. Little Ed suddenly exploded in a wallow of tears, sobs, intense anguish, and a deep, deep dredging of everything in him that could feel. He cried and cried and cried. He didn't know for how long. Then finally, he was still.

As he raised himself at long last he was looking directly into the wolf's eyes. "I didn't know there was that much mourning left in me," Little Ed said to the wolf.

"You had mourned the passing of Golden Bear fully," replied the wolf, "but when Golden Bear died there was a part of you that died as well. You had not yet mourned that part of yourself. That is why we brought you here."

A sudden knowing dawned on Little Ed, about the interconnectedness of all beings.

"Who are you?" asked Little Ed of the wolf.

"That would be difficult to explain," said the wolf, "what matters is *why* I am here. Now that you have mourned your own dying, it is appropriate that the cub and I merge together."

The wolf walked over to where the cub was standing and they blended together with ease. Little Ed blinked.

Something was changing. The place where they had merged together was growing larger and becoming more dense but with a soft glow to it.

"Who are you?" asked Little Ed, just as the final form was taking shape. No answer was needed. Standing in its fullness and gently glowing was Little Ed's new heart animal, a golden bear.

The Final Carving

Little Ed returned to the tree where it had fallen, where Golden Bear had died. He returned there day after day, carrying his tools and working on the tree.

Now with his new heart animal, the golden bear, he found himself to have boundless energy, and he knew the totem pole needed to be finished. The carving happened almost of its own accord, fluidly, skillfully, knowingly. He had originally had some question about how the golden sunlight and the tree would both be carved into a totem pole, but now there were no questions nor any doubt. And although he had no idea how they would be carved, he knew they would and that they would be exactly as they needed to be.

His movements were crisp and direct, there was no longer any debate in him about things. He either knew or he didn't know and he was completely at home with both. Not knowing didn't cause him to halt and knowing did not result in arrogance. They were both merely facts on the path of his being.

His animals were with him almost all the time now,

if not immediately visible, at least present in their feeling. He interacted with them freely and they were at home making any comments they needed to, especially concerning the carving.

As Little Ed carved, the animals emerged easily and fluidly from the tree. Their form was evident and Little Ed was surprised to see how many eyes they embodied. The mountain lion at the base had eyes in his ears and in his heart, as well as a small eye in each claw. The flying horse had a huge eye in each of his wings. He had also become transparent now, although Little Ed found no way to carve that aspect into the totem pole. His solar plexus animal, the golden lion, always carried a great sense of ease, and this was fully expressed in his demeanor in the totem pole. The golden bear, his new heart animal, stood forth almost luminously, and contained the most eyes of any of the animals. There was a particularly large eye in his belly. The bird was carved in full flight, with his wings outstretched, each also with a large eye. Since Little Ed had emerged from the passageway, whenever he saw his throat animal, it was flying in tandem with his white horse, and they were beautifully coordinated in their movements.

It was most fascinating for him to watch his forehead tree emerge in the carving. Its roots wove downward throughout the totem pole, so that they were in intimate contact with each of the animals below. The main tap root wove itself playfully into the mountain lion's hind legs and feet, a branch of it blended softly into the flying horse's mane, and a third branch of it merged with the golden lion's tail. And other roots went into the golden bear's ears and the bird's wings. The trunk stood mighty and massive, with a single eye at its center, and above, its branches spread gently embracing a series of solar discs which contained the sunshine of Little Ed's crown.

The entire totem pole was fluid and beautifully carved, and when he was done Little Ed dug a deep hole in the place where Golden Bear had died. He then took a long pole and pried and raised the totem pole until its lower portion was anchored in that hole and it stood tall and strong as a guardian of that spot where his beautiful old friend had died.

Now he was done. Little Ed knelt in front of the totem pole, thanking it for bringing him on this journey, asking it to watch over the spot where Golden Bear had departed, and asking it for any advice it had to give him.

"I gladly stand here on this sacred spot," said the totem pole, "and watch over the doorway through which your dear friend has gone. If you should ever return you will find me here. The doorway is a doorway of beauty, and when you are called, go through it as courageously as your friend did. Your journey with me has been a full one and you have changed in incomprehensible ways. Carry the love that has grown in you into everything you do, it is a beautiful signature of your friend's passing. And there is one more thing he would like for you to carry with you."

The Return

Little Ed took the train from one station to the next, stopping whenever he felt like it, for a day or two, to spend time with the town or the terrain, feeling a need to know the country in which he lived.

He met people casually and talked to them, he visited craftspeople wherever he could, he ate lightly and sparingly, and slept well in the hostels or homes of friends he had just met.

He had no sense of how long it took, feeling a need only to experience as much of this country as he could on his way back home. Occasionally a memory would waft through his mind and he was always amazed at how different he felt now, of how much he had changed from the boy who first set out on the journey over two years ago.

Wherever he was, whether travelling through the mountains or the plains or along the seashore, he tried to absorb as fully as possible the events and smells, the people and words, the flavor and substance of this vast country.

His home town seemed so different when he arrived,

unannounced and unanticipated. It seemed so much smaller and somehow too protected. There was no place in it for much adventure, and he knew he would not be staying here for long.

He knocked at the door of the home where he had lived, almost as if he were a stranger stopping to ask directions.

His little sister, Susan, bigger now, opened the door and stared at him for a few seconds, then she said excitedly as she flung her arms around his neck, "Little Ed! Little Ed! Little Ed! We had no idea where you were!"

He embraced her warmly, looked lovingly into her eyes, and gently said, "My name is no longer Little Ed. I am now called Golden Bear."

Appendix

The Beginning

No one really knew how, when or where it began. Many theorists tried to pinpoint a beginning, while at the same time others saw the process as having been continuous. In a strange way both theories were true. Whatever it was that had preceded it and led into it, there was no doubting now that changes were occurring at an unbelievable rate.

Some attributed the sudden changes to the rise of the personal computer which gave everyone the capacity to educate themselves and to have immediate access to all available information. Others saw it as stemming from the ultimate failure of an educational system which had been originally structured for training people to be content in boring and repetitive industrial jobs.

Some felt it was even due to the massive spread of television which provided people with a window continually open to ways of being which extended beyond any particular culture, engendering a postcultural perspective that brought people back to an earnest consideration of the individual person, and thus to the uniqueness of being.

Still there were others who attributed it to the sudden openness of a deeply feeling people who had been imprisoned in a giant feudal system for seventy years, the openness spreading like electricity from one country to the next until the entire world was involved in what the United States had originally felt was its own flowering: the freedom to communicate openly and honestly, only to discover that *it* was one of those most behind the times, and that its governmental structure had involved deceit and criminality that was finally beginning to be uncovered and truly spoken about.

Still others saw it as a synthesis, the merging of thesis and antithesis, the union of opposites into a new and superordinate way of knowing and being, which far surpassed the duality in which opposing parties had long been frozen.

And there were those who knew that it could only be the result of the spread of meditation around the world, ultimately culminating in the growth of consciousness to a new plane which would involve society in its own evolution in a way and at a rate without precedent.

Those of a more psychological nature understood that it was the result of finally having given the Unconscious its due, thus listening to it and letting it become involved in the redressing of a heretofore unbalanced psychological orientation.

And then there were the New Politicos, who were convinced it had come about as the result of the change in presidential power, ending the reign of two disastrous presidencies that had done what they could to divide the country between impoverished people and the shamelessly wealthy, where money had been transferred from most social programs, including education, into large commercial corporations, plunging the country into previously unheard of debt and greed. The new president had, through restructuring the taxation system, put a cap on possible income, thus ending years of greedy speculation and shameless profiteering.

One of the early steps originated in the realization that the two extremes of societal rejection, children and elders, those with no obvious economic contribution, needed each other. So the Elder Link program was born. In this program, the youngest children, those not yet in school and particularly those of working parents, were brought to spend the day with the elderly and retired. The differences were immediately noticeable: the children became much more settled and less needy; since there were plenty of elderly to go around, every child got all the attention it needed. And secondly, physical problems in the elderly underwent an immediate drop. The elders seemed to be rejuvenated by their relationships with the young children. Initially they complained about how difficult it was, but soon their vitality returned and they found themselves capable of doing much more than they had imagined they could at that age. They had become so used to being dependent that they had not realized how it debilitated them. But what startled most economists was that the expense of maintaining both the elderly and the young plummeted significantly. Medical costs almost disappeared along with lengthy illnesses in both groups. The elderly were much healthier up until the day of their deaths. And their deaths were not hidden from the children. Children were taken to the services, allowed to say goodbye, and were attendant at the burial.

Sociologists also noted that the children were much more mature when they began their formal schooling and they appeared to have a much more profound connection with the family and society. Social problems at school were lessened and for those that did occur, some elderly "companions" were maintained: older people who were willing to be available to students experiencing difficulties. The interesting thing about this development was that it was found that those elders who were not given any instructions did much better than those who were coached or taught specific ways to be with the student. Somehow the sincere presence of the elder was much more important to the student than any specific thing that the elder did. In fact, it came to be appreciated that the elders had such a rich store of experience to draw upon in being with the students that any specific orientation tended to limit them. Furthermore, the elders were also enriched by this relationship and by their own discovery of the creativity that emerged from them in particularly trying circumstances with the students.

The elder companions had such a lasting influence on the maturity of the students that this program was expanded until it was made a specific aspect of schooling. At the beginning each student was given one afternoon each week to spend with an elder. Some elders would work in the garden with the student, others would take them to a museum or an art gallery. Many would just sit and talk, or have tea or milk with the students. Still others would bring the students gradually into their own interests: a lawyer would take the student to a court trial, a craftsman would involve the student in his craft, a businessman in his business. This orientation so enriched the students that eventually it was combined in a highly serious way with the findings of the bio-socio-historians.

This small and specialized group had arrived at the view that the primary social problems in modern industrial societies originated from a synthetic prolonged adolescence. All organisms, they argued, arrive at a biological time in their lives when it is imperative that the offspring leave off being a child and become independent from their parents. In rhesus monkeys the separation occurs at about six months of age, and is enacted by both the offspring and the mother. If the young monkey does not leave it will be driven off by its mother. In all animals this separation occurs instinctively and naturally. In the human it should occur biologically shortly after puberty, that is around age twelve or fourteen.

But humans had been living in such a way that leaving home at this age when it would have been biologically natural was socially discouraged and financially impossible. Children were expected to be supported by thier families. But it was not until the true financial expense became evident, the high school dropouts that eventually became dependent upon a welfare system for the rest of their lives, the runaways, the teenage suicides, the young addicts, that the bio-socio-historians began to be taken seriously. They had proposed that a gap be allowed in a student's education, a time when the student could, in fact, leave home and go on a year or two of adventure, sustained by the government through youth hostels and free travel privileges, particularly on trains. This, it was proposed, would revive the stagnant railroad industry. (Indeed, it was believed by many that the bio-socio-historians had been carefully groomed by the railroad corporations to come up with exactly this finding). It was predicted that students who were allowed such a time of adventure would return to school much more mature than those who had not been allowed this opportunity.

This proposition was supported fully by the elders, who added the proviso that students be encouraged to undertake one or several apprenticeships with an elder during that time. Numerous teachers supported this proposition as well, and even though a fairly vocal opposition developed, fearing for the lives and welfare of the students, funding was provided by Congress for an experimental approach, comparing a small group of students who were allowed this "Wandertime" (as it came to be called) with all the students who were not. The results of the study were stunning and could not be denied. All students involved in the experimental program became successful in their lives. Not by any academic standard, but in terms of the dedication with which they applied themselves and their contentment in their chosen professions. Academicians were surprised by the number who chose to be craftspeople. None of the students who participated in the experimental program were subsequently involved in any legal conflicts.

The results were so significant that legislators, teachers, and law enforcement personnel began an immediate push to have this program instituted around the country. But the biggest support came from the students themselves. They were enthusiastically behind it. A sigh of relief could be heard around the country. People were simultaneously aware that something had been terribly out of place and now it was beginning to come back into its natural balance.

This was the beginning of a return to a much more organic way of being. Ceremony began once again to be seriously engaged in, not as a social requirement but as the true demarcation of a change in the state of one's being, or a reaching for the greater depths within oneself. The shift from outer to inner had begun, and people began to realize more and more that the state of the world was but a reflection of their inner state and that the only way to change the world was to move consistently toward a place of wholeness within themselves. Deep feelings began to become more valued than the superficial action that had so long been dominant. And guidance from the archetypal realm came to be relied upon as the ultimate guidance along one's path in the world.

Author's Epilogue

If I felt that you, the reader, would take this work as a mere novel describing a possible future for education I would not have written it. The fact is that such a possibility exists right now.

The Ceremony of Severance was adapted from the current beautiful work of Kia Wood who takes adolescents out on their first Vision Quest, helping them go through that natural passageway of being birthed into the young adults that they are. Often the parents need more help in this than the child, unwilling as they are to face the pain and joy of letting go, having themselves frequently been the offspring of parents who clung to them in ownership.

The possibility of this great country beginning to provide support for our children exists now, if we were only to concern ourselves more with the creativity of the people who are emerging, i.e., the children, than with the defense and protection from our imagined enemies. We are nationally neurotic, destroying ourselves economically in the support of a massive military while our people go hungry and homeless and our children grow up in the profound experience of being rejected in their own homeland. The domination of our Government by entrenched economic interests rather than by the individuals who live here is the most shameful thing we have ever allowed.

The critical views of "school" in this novel have already been made in numerous talks and writings, and much more eloquently, by John Taylor Gatto, to name but one. Frequently the problem is not the individual teachers, many of whom would love to be able to truly teach. The difficulty is usually a strangulating administration overly concerned with its own perpetuation. But certainly not all schools are like this. My daughter attends a remarkable school in which individual creativity is supremely valued and other curricular aspects are woven into that.

The possibilities of utilizing computerized interactive video as a mechanism for teaching children things of a more factual nature, like mathematics, (rather than the things which would involve them in an awareness of their own unique *process,*) is certainly demonstrated by current video games. Much of the factual knowledge that a child should acquire could easily be structured into progressive games that the child could involve him or herself in at the appropriate motivational or developmental moment. Some of our most creative minds are leading this development and they have not necessarily been the successful products of our schools.

The value of apprenticeship seems to be something our European forebears wanted to leave behind, perhaps wanting to sever themselves from their cultural and economic roots as much as they severed themselves from the reverence for the earth and nature, refusing the examples of their Native American hosts. Perhaps this is why they fought so hard to disconnect the Native Americans from their own traditions and ways of honoring. Apprenticeship is so much more than just learning something that another teaches. It provides the thread of life and continuity from one generation to the next. It provides a situation where a youth can be nurtured and appreciated by an elder. It provides a place where the young can allow their creativity to grow within the nest of caring and supervision by someone who has already traversed the path of growing.

Although Little Ed's meetings with his chakra animals is put forth here in semi-fictional form, there are numerous people who can testify to the deep transformational properties of having an ongoing relationship with them. Work with the chakra animals in the Personal Totem Pole Process and with the Animals of the Four Windows of Knowing has been ongoing for over a decade, and the people who have taken it as a path know its profound power to bring a person back home to their true center. Rather than taking someone else's word for who or how we are to be, or conforming to the theoretical views of the teacher or therapist, the chakra animals embody a guidance that comes from deep within each individual, and conducts us through our own experience into that being we originally are.

We have spent too many generations training people to disregard the most important window of all: that which is concerned with individual healing and wholeness. The Council of Animals provides a way of balancing our various energies, of helping them heal individually in places where they have been injured, and of helping them come together around a single center, this being one of the ways in which it differs from more traditional shamanic journeying. A second significant difference is that it provides a framework that begins the integration of the four windows of knowing. The fact that the chakra system exists in all four windows provides a known doorway for entering, and a way of anchoring and understanding deep imagery

The potential for truly coming home to the guidance that exists in the remarkable organism that we are, inherently so, is available to every person right now.

This is the beginning.